W9-COI-251

THE HARDY BOYS® MYSTERY STORIES

90 3094 29 040

The HARDY BOYS®

DANGER ON THE DIAMOND

FRANKLIN W. DIXON

A MINSTREL® BOOK

PUBLISHED BY POCKET BOOKS

New York   London   Toronto   Sydney   Tokyo

84774

A MINSTREL PAPERBACK *ORIGINAL*

 A Minstrel Book published by
POCKET BOOKS, a division of Simon & Schuster, Inc.,
1230 Avenue of the Americas, New York, N.Y. 10020

ISBN: 0-671-63425-9

First Minstrel Books printing May, 1988

10 9 8 7 6 5 4 3 2 1

Contents

DANGER ON
THE DIAMOND

1 Bleacher Breakdown

"Oh, no!" cried Joe Hardy. Caught in a rundown, he was desperately trying to get back to first base.

As the second baseman threw to first, Joe froze in his tracks. The momentary hesitation was all the first baseman needed. Reaching out, he tried to brush Joe with his glove. Joe twisted his body to avoid him, but he wasn't fast enough. He was tagged out three feet from first base.

"Nice try, kid," said Zeke "Fireball" Horner, the ex-pitching great, who had just picked him off. "But you telegraphed your steal. Pay attention out here. If you daydream, you're out."

Joe walked back to the dugout and sat down next to his older brother, Frank. He ran his

1

fingers through his blond hair and shook his head. "I can't believe I let myself get picked off," he said in a disgusted voice. "I'm a better base runner than that."

"Cool down," replied Frank. "Even major leaguers get into that situation sometimes."

"That's true," admitted Joe. "And besides, this is only the first day of baseball camp. I guess I'm just too impatient."

Frank rolled his eyes. "So, what else is new," he said with a grin.

The Hardy brothers were a year apart in age and were totally different types. Seventeen-year-old, blond, blue-eyed Joe tended to be slightly impulsive and hot-tempered, while brown-haired, brown-eyed Frank was thoughtful and coolheaded.

Frank nudged his brother. "I know how you can get a jump on Horner," he said.

"How?" asked Joe. "By starting my steal the night before?"

Frank shook his head, then said, "I noticed that after Horner looks the runner back, he goes into his pitching motion, completely ignoring the guy on base. He throws a wicked fast ball, but it takes him two and a half seconds to deliver the pitch once he begins his motion."

"Are you sure about that?"

Frank showed his brother a stopwatch. "The numbers don't lie," he said.

"That's good enough for me," said Joe. He jogged out to the field and convinced Horner to let him try again. As he stood on first base, he gave his brother the thumbs-up sign. He stole second three pitches later.

Horner gave Joe an approving nod. Joe returned to the dugout with a large smile on his face. "Thanks for the tip, Frank."

"Don't mention it," replied his brother.

Joe sat back and sighed contentedly. "This is a great way to spend part of the summer," he said. "Spike Nolan's baseball camp is terrific. We're really learning a lot."

"We're lucky Nolan decided to come to Bayport this summer," commented Frank.

Spike Nolan, a former big-league catcher, traveled around the country with a small staff of ex-major leaguers offering instruction on the finer points of the game of baseball.

When the Hardys and their good friends Biff Hooper and Tony Prito had learned that Nolan was coming to Bayport, they'd jumped at the chance to better their baseball skills. Most of their teammates on the Bayport Bombers, their high school baseball team, were also taking part in the month-long session.

Frank and Joe watched Horner give a pitching exhibition. The southpaw had a strong arm, and the ball was a blur when it left his hand. It was easy to see how Horner had earned his nickname, Fireball.

Spike Nolan called for everyone to meet him on the mound. Nolan was a short, slightly overweight man in his late forties. He had a curly mop of grayish brown hair, which stuck out from beneath his cap.

"Okay, pitchers, listen up," he said. "You'll throw against Hammer Carter, our batting instructor." A stringy beanpole of a man stood at home plate casually knocking the clay from his spikes with the handle of his bat.

"He doesn't look so tough," Frank said as he studied the batter. "Wonder why they call him Hammer?"

"I wouldn't worry about it," Joe said. "These ballplayers all have nicknames. It's probably a joke. That guy's so skinny he can barely lift the bat off his shoulder. Use your fastball on him. He won't have a chance."

Nolan studied a list of pitchers. "Frank Hardy," he said. "You're first." He tossed Frank the ball.

"Here's the situation," Nolan said. "The bases are loaded. It's the bottom of the ninth. The seventh game of the World Series. Your team leads by three runs. There are two outs and the batter has three hits in this game already. You have to get him out."

Frank dug his fingers into the seams of the ball. Nolan put on his catching gear and walked out to the mound.

"Okay, Frank," he said with a smile. "What are your best pitches?"

"Fastball and curve."

"Okay. Watch my signs. Two fingers for curve and one for fastball. You got a slider?"

"Sure, but it's not that good."

"I'll be the judge of that. Slider is three. Let's see what you can do."

4

Nolan planted himself behind the plate and flashed Frank the sign for the fastball. He held up his glove to receive Frank's pitch.

Frank grinned. I'll blow it right by Carter, he thought. He reared up and fired.

Crack! Frank watched his best pitch roar high into the air. It landed four hundred feet away. Nolan flashed another sign. This time he wanted the curveball. Frank wound up and fired the ball over the plate. *Crack!* That ball zoomed even farther than the first pitch.

Frank's stomach twisted into a knot as Hammer blasted his best pitches into orbit. Spike Nolan walked to the mound and took the baseball from Frank. "Okay, Frank. You can take a break now." He called out another name.

As Frank walked slowly to the dugout, he shook his head and pounded his glove with his hand. "Did you see that?" he asked his brother.

"That guy really creamed you," Joe said. "What did you give him?"

"My best stuff. He pounded my fastball like it was coming in slow motion. He wasn't fooled by my curve. I got him on the slider, though. He only hit that one for a single."

"Don't worry about it," Joe said. "You'll find a way to strike him out."

The Hardys watched the other pitchers take turns trying to nail Hammer Carter. Then Spike Nolan called for batting practice. "Come on," Joe said. "Biff is up first. He'll show this Nolan guy what the Bombers can do!"

5

But Biff Hooper, the tall, muscular, hard-hitting center fielder for the Bombers, struck out five times against Horner. And when he took the field, he missed nearly every ball that was hit to him.

Frank and Joe walked back to the dugout with Biff. He was muttering angrily to himself and kicking at tufts of grass.

"Calm down," said Tony Prito, who was walking back with them. "You're so hot you could fry an egg on your forehead."

"It's easy for you to say," replied Biff. "You haven't looked bad yet—at bat or in the field. Almost everybody else out here looks terrible."

"Lighten up, Biff," Tony said. "It's only a game. You should learn to relax. I mean, life's full of little problems. Like this baseball here."

He tossed the ball in the air, catching it with his right hand. Then he picked up four more baseballs from the bench. Soon he was juggling the five balls easily.

"It doesn't pay to let things bother you." As he juggled, he puffed out his cheeks and crossed his eyes.

Biff laughed and shook his head. "You're a real clown, Prito."

"Who, me?" Tony kept throwing the balls higher and higher in the air. "Now, pay attention," he said. "It's all mind over matter. See how easily I'm juggling these four balls?"

"You've got five there," said Joe.

"What? I can't juggle five balls at once. It's impossible." Tony covered his head with his

6

hands and dropped to the ground as the baseballs fell in a shower around him.

Biff and the Hardys looked down at their friend and laughed.

"Thanks, Tony," Biff said. "I feel a lot better."

"Hey, no problem." Tony got to his feet. "What are friends for?"

After each player had taken a turn at batting, Spike Nolan called for everyone's attention. "Okay, guys, we had a good workout. Now let's get over to the bleachers. I want to talk to all of you."

Spike Nolan had arranged to set up his baseball camp at Bayport High. The school's field contained two diamonds, and the players had access to the gym's locker room. Nolan's trailer served as the camp's office. It occupied a corner of the parking lot, next to the field.

The players filed into the stands behind first base while Nolan conferred with Horner and Carter. Then the three instructors handed out evaluations to each player. Immediately, everyone began to talk to each other about the results.

"All right, settle down," Nolan said. "As you look at those papers, you'll see that my instructors and I have rated each of you on your pitching, hitting, fielding, and base-running skills, with numbers from one to ten. One being the best. And ten being the worst."

"Hey, Mr. Nolan," called Tony Prito.

"What is it, Tony?" Nolan said.

"How come I got an eight in my fielding? I caught everything Mr. Carter hit to me."

7

"You made all the hard catches, but a simple dribbler went right by you. A good ball player is supposed to make the easy plays. You need work. All of you do. But that's the purpose of this camp. We want you to make mistakes. That's how you learn." He looked at Tony. "Understand?"

Tony grinned and nodded. He tossed his glove into the air. It fell through his hands onto the bleacher seat right below him. As he reached over to pick it up, he accidentally kicked it through an opening in the bleachers onto the ground. He climbed down from the stands.

Joe raised his hand.

"What is it?" asked Nolan.

"Mr. Nolan, we already know how to play baseball. We just want to play it better."

"Your name's Joe Hardy, right?"

Joe nodded. "Right."

"Okay, Joe. We know you came to this camp because you want to play better baseball. That's why we made it pretty tough for you out here today. But you are going to get better. Why? Because my instructors and I are going to teach you everything we know."

Nolan put his hands behind his back and paced in front of the bleachers. "This camp will be tough. But if you don't quit, I guarantee that you'll have the best baseball team in this area."

Nolan looked hard at the group. "What's the name of your team?" he called out.

"The Bombers!" everyone shouted.

"Let's hear it again, louder this time!"

"The Bombers!!"

8

"Again!" yelled Nolan.

"THE BOMBERS!!"

"That's right," Nolan shouted. "You're the Bombers, and you're going to win every game you play. And I'm going to teach you how to win. We're going to train hard, and you're going to be the best you can be."

Frank and Joe and the others waved their arms over their heads and cheered. They chanted the team's name over and over again, "Bombers! Bombers!" As they stomped their feet on the stands, the bleachers began to vibrate.

Suddenly, the stands began weaving back and forth. A grinding shriek of twisting metal drowned out the chorus of cheers. The bleachers began to slide forward.

"Nobody move!" yelled Frank.

But his warning came too late. The players began leaping from the stands. Before everyone could make it safely to the ground, the bleachers collapsed!

2 Wild Pitches

"Biff, would you mind getting your spikes out of my face?" Frank asked in a muffled voice.

Biff lifted his foot slightly, mumbling something that sounded like "Sorry." Seconds later, a pair of arms reached inside and pulled Biff free. Then it was Frank's turn.

"Have you seen my brother?" Frank asked Hammer Carter, who had pulled him out. The batting instructor shook his head, too busy even to talk. Frank looked around frantically for Joe among the tangle of bodies struggling to get out from under the collapsed bleachers. Then he saw a familiar-looking T-shirt. Reaching into the wreckage, he untangled his brother from two other guys.

Joe smiled at Frank. "What took you so long?" he asked.

"Are you okay?"

"I'm fine. Just a little stiff," Joe said, rubbing his arm. He stared at the bleachers. "Those stands are pretty sturdy, and there were only fifteen of us sitting in them. How could they collapse?"

"I don't know, but I think we ought to find out," replied Frank. "Come on, let's help get people out of there."

Twenty minutes later, everyone had been pulled free. Many of them had bumps and bruises, but no one seemed to be seriously injured.

Spike Nolan was about to send everyone home for the day when Chief Collig of the Bayport police, accompanied by one of his officers, came into view. He introduced himself and the officer to Spike Nolan, then asked, "What's going on here?"

"We just had a little accident," replied Nolan. "It was no big deal, Chief."

Chief Collig rose to his full height and stared at Nolan. "Any so-called accidents that happen in my town are a big deal, Mr. Nolan," he said. He narrowed his eyes. "It's a good thing Officer Larsen and I happened to be riding by. Now, I'd like to hear exactly what happened."

While Chief Collig talked to Nolan, Frank and Joe poked around the wrecked bleachers, looking for clues. After a few minutes of searching, Frank found something. Jutting from the locking mechanism was a bent wire hanger. He showed it

11

to Joe, who nodded. The Hardys walked over to Chief Collig and Spike Nolan.

"Excuse me, Chief, Mr. Nolan," interrupted Frank, "but I think we found something."

The chief raised his eyebrows. "Let me take a look at it," he said.

Frank handed him the hanger. "This was sticking in the locking mechanism of the bleachers."

Chief Collig fingered the hanger. His forehead wrinkled as he concentrated on its odd, twisted shape. "Very interesting. But what's the point?"

"It looks like somebody rigged the lock. Why don't you dust it for prints?"

Chief Collig sighed and shook his head. "That would be a waste of time. Any prints there might have been would have been smudged when you pulled the hanger out." He returned the hanger to Frank. "But thanks for the help, anyway."

Officer Larsen walked over to them. "Everyone seems to be okay, Chief, outside of a few bumps and bruises. Looks like an accident."

"What about the hanger in the lock?" Frank pressed.

The chief was about to reply when a burst of laughter rang out. The chief turned around and saw Tony Prito standing on the pitcher's mound. He was juggling three baseballs, his glove, and his cap in front of an appreciative audience of some of his teammates.

"Tony's always kidding around," said Joe.

"Is that so?" the chief replied.

Joe nodded and grinned. "He likes making

12

people laugh. You should see some of the practical jokes he's played. They're a riot."

The chief looked thoughtful. "Where was he when the bleachers fell down?" he asked.

"He was in the stands with the rest of us," said Frank.

Joe looked at his brother and shook his head slowly. "No, he wasn't," he said. "I saw him climb down underneath the stands just before they caved in."

"Now that's very interesting." The chief rubbed his chin. "If I were a guy who loved practical jokes, this would be a great gag."

He walked over to Tony, followed by the Hardys and Spike Nolan. "It must have been pretty funny when the bleachers collapsed," Chief Collig said to Tony.

"I wasn't laughing, Chief," said Tony, as he continued to juggle. "They nearly fell on my head."

"What were you doing under the stands?"

"Getting my glove. I dropped it."

"Did you take a hanger with you?"

Tony let the balls, glove, and cap drop onto the ground. He stared at Chief Collig. "Huh? What are you talking about, Chief?"

The police chief gave a huge sigh. "Okay, Tony, have it your own way. But no more funny stuff from now on."

"Wait a minute, Chief," protested Frank. "Sure, Tony plays practical jokes. But he wouldn't do anything like that."

13

"Give me a break," Tony said. "I didn't do anything. I just went to pick up my glove."

The chief gave Tony a hard look. Then he shifted his gaze to Frank. "You said it yourself, Frank. Somebody jammed a hanger into the lock on the stands. Tony was underneath the bleachers just before they fell down. It all adds up."

Frank shook his head. "No, it doesn't. It's circumstantial evidence. You don't have any proof. Or any witnesses."

"I've got my instincts. And they tell me that Tony played a practical joke that went bad. He's lucky no one was seriously hurt." He turned and faced Tony. "But hear this, young man. If there are any more accidents at this camp, I'll know just where to look."

The chief nodded at Nolan and said, "Stay in touch." Then he and Officer Larsen headed back to their squad car.

Tapping the hanger on his palm, Frank watched Larsen and the chief drive away.

"What do you think?" Joe asked his brother.

"I think we have the makings of a case. Let's keep our eyes open and see what we can find out."

They headed for the locker room to shower and change. Afterward, as they walked to the parking lot and their van, they saw Tony and Biff arguing.

"I didn't do it, Biff," said Tony.

"That's not what the chief thinks," Biff said hotly. "You know, I hurt my hand when I fell.

14

How am I going to be a better hitter if I can't hold a bat?"

Joe moved between Biff and Tony. "Take it easy, guys."

Biff leaned forward past Joe and lightly jabbed Tony's chest with his finger. "Just watch yourself, Tony," he said. "Sometimes you take your jokes too far."

"You're making a mistake, Biff," said Frank.

"No, I'm not. I saw Tony leave the stands. Next thing I know, I'm falling down. It wasn't funny, Tony."

Tony held out his hands in protest. "Come on, Biff. I wouldn't do anything like that."

"Tell that to my hand," said Biff. He tried to wriggle his fingers, then winced in pain. "It hurts."

"My arm's a little stiff," Joe said to Biff. "But you don't see me picking on Tony. Give him a break. He's your friend. Why would he try to hurt you?"

"I'm not saying he did it on purpose. Just that he should be more careful when he plays jokes." Biff stormed away rubbing his hand.

Tony looked gratefully at Frank and Joe. "Thanks a lot, guys. I'm glad somebody here believes me."

"Don't worry about Biff," Frank said. "He'll cool down in the morning."

"I hope so," said Tony. Reaching into his pocket, he pulled out a battered wristwatch. "Uh-oh. I've got to get going. I've got pizzas to

15

deliver. Thanks again, guys. See you tomorrow."
He ran off toward his car.

Frank looked at the hanger in his hands and shook his head. "Tony wouldn't mess up the bleachers. I know he wouldn't."

"Right," agreed Joe. "But somebody did. The question is—who?"

Frank looked at his brother. "That's the first question," he said grimly. "The second question is—*why*?"

Early the next morning, Frank shook his brother awake.

Joe groaned and pulled the covers over his head. "Leave me alone. It's summer vacation, remember?"

"We have baseball camp, remember?" replied Frank. "Your alarm didn't go off, so I thought I'd better wake you up."

Joe sat up, rubbing the sleep from his eyes. "Ow," he said. "I'm stiff all over. You know, I've got a black-and-blue mark on my leg where Josh Webster fell on me yesterday. How do you feel?"

"I feel great." Frank did ten quick push-ups. "Can you beat that?"

"Give me a break, will you?" Joe yawned and peered sleepily at his clock. "It's only six-thirty."

"Camp starts at seven-thirty. We've got to get going." Frank headed for the door. "I'll be down in the kitchen."

Joe jumped out of bed and washed and dressed quickly. The house was quiet. The Hardys' fa-

16

ther, Fenton, a well-known private detective, was out of town on a case. Their mother, Laura, and their aunt Gertrude, Fenton's sister, who lived with the Hardys, were still asleep.

Joe ran downstairs to the kitchen. Frank was sitting at the table drinking a glass of orange juice. A plate full of whole-grain toast and two bowls piled high with multigrain cereal sat in front of him.

"What are you doing?" asked Joe. "We don't have time for breakfast."

Frank lowered his glass. "Take it easy. We've got plenty of time. Besides, if we don't eat breakfast, we won't have enough energy to get through the day."

"You sound just like Mom."

"She's right." Frank shoved one of the cereal bowls in Joe's direction. "Here, I poured you some of that new Power! cereal. It has a full day's supply of all the vitamins and minerals your body needs."

Joe rolled his eyes. "Now you sound just like a TV commercial!"

After breakfast, the Hardys headed out the door to their dark blue police van. The van had been given to Frank and Joe by Chief Collig after they had solved the *Desert Phantom* case. Although it wasn't new, the van was in good condition. The brothers had repainted it, and they planned to install a CB radio and other equipment in it sometime in the future.

When Frank and Joe arrived at the baseball

camp, they were put in a group headed by Hammer Carter. Today, he was going to show them the finer points of hitting.

Carter took his group to the batting cage nearest the dugout. On the pitcher's mound was a large machine that looked like a tractor. Hammer took a box of baseballs and fed them into a funnel that stuck up from the rear of the machine.

"This is a pitching machine," he told them. "It has three speeds. And I'm going to use it to test your hitting skills. Who wants to be first?"

Grabbing a bat, Tony Prito positioned himself in the batter's box. Carter adjusted the speed setting and stepped away. The machine released a ball. Tony swung and missed. Ten pitches later, he still hadn't hit the ball.

Tony dropped his bat, then began to do a tap dance on home plate. While he danced, he caught the last few balls that the machine spit out. Nobody laughed at Tony's antics.

When Tony realized he wasn't getting any laughs, he stopped dancing. He gave a shrug and picked up his bat. "I guess you guys just don't have a sense of humor," he said in a casual voice, and stepped out of the batter's box.

"Okay, who's next?" asked Carter.

"Let's see what I can do," said Joe. He hustled up to the plate, got into a comfortable position, and nodded his head. Carter fed in some baseballs and stepped away.

Joe did terrifically, spraying the pitches all over the field. He took a few wild swings, but, all in all, Carter seemed impressed with Joe's hitting ability.

"Not bad," he said. "Who's next? Frank?"

Frank didn't do as well as his brother. The first pitch came in, and Frank took a mighty swing. But his timing was off—the ball swished past him.

The last ball whizzed by him. Frank was stunned. Struck out by a machine, he thought. Carter eased the bat from his hands, then stood in the batter's box.

"Look, here's what you're doing wrong," he said. "You've got a good, full swing, but your concentration is off. You're misjudging the speed of the ball—and swinging too early. Put a couple of balls in the machine and I'll show you."

Frank loaded up the mechanical pitcher, and Hammer blasted every pitch deep into the outfield. As Frank watched, he realized that Carter never took his eyes off the ball.

After lunch, Frank and Joe worked with Nolan and Horner on their fielding. Frank tried to get back to the batting cage all afternoon, but there was never enough time. At the end of the day's session, everyone crowded around Spike Nolan. He handed out team rosters to each player.

"I've divided you into two teams," Nolan said. "Starting tomorrow, you'll spend half the day in instruction and the other half competing against each other in practice games. Any questions?" There were none. "That's it for today. See you tomorrow at seven-thirty."

19

Nolan started back toward his trailer. Frank ran after him. "Mr. Nolan?"

"What is it, Frank?" Nolan asked, turning around.

"Would you mind if I use the pitching machine one more time before I leave today?"

Nolan smiled at Frank. "Can't you wait until tomorrow morning? It will still be here."

"I know that," Frank said with a nod. "But I never got a chance to use Mr. Carter's suggestions. I'm a good hitter. I just want a little extra practice."

"Okay, you can use the machine," Nolan said. "But only for ten pitches."

"Thanks!" said Frank, grinning. He ran off to get his bat.

Joe and Biff Hooper went with Frank to the batting cage. On the way, they passed Zeke Horner, who was sorting through a box of baseballs. He looked up as they passed and said, "Nice work on your slider today, Frank. It's really coming along." He picked up the box of balls, gave the three of them a friendly nod, and walked away.

Frank loaded the machine while Joe and Biff played catch. As they tossed the ball around, Tony Prito walked over to them.

Waiting for the first pitch to come in, Frank remembered Carter's instructions. He slammed the first ball deep into the outfield.

"Good shot, Frank," said Joe as he watched his brother hit. "I knew you could do it."

Frank slammed the next pitch just as far. It

seemed as though his bat had eyes. Frank blasted the next pitches high into the air.

"All *right!*" said Joe, clapping his hands in approval. "Ten pitches and ten perfect hits."

Frank turned around to smile at his brother. As he did, the machine suddenly spit another pitch at him. It zipped past his right ear. Frank turned back to stare at the machine, and another ball came straight at him, slamming into his shoulder. Almost at the same time, a third pitch zoomed toward his head!

3 Explosive Discussions

Stunned by the blow, Frank collapsed slowly onto the ground.

"Frank!" Joe dropped his glove and raced over to his brother. Biff Hooper and Tony Prito ran to the machine and tried to shut it off, but it was jammed.

Together they put their shoulders to the machine and used all their strength to push it on its side. When the machine struck the ground, it made a grinding noise, then stopped.

Meanwhile, Joe was bending anxiously over his brother. Frank sat up slowly, holding his head. With Joe's help, he managed to get to his feet. After a few steps, his knees buckled, and he would have fallen to the ground again if Joe hadn't caught him.

"Take it easy, Frank," Joe said. "Here, sit down." He eased his brother onto the grass. Turning to Biff, he said, "Go tell Nolan what happened."

Biff ran off. Tony came over and sat down next to Frank. "That was the strangest thing I've ever seen," Tony said.

"I don't know what happened," mumbled Frank. "One minute I was taking batting practice, then it turned out to be target practice. Ow, my head hurts." He lowered his head into his hands.

"Can you stand up?" asked Joe.

"I think so," said Frank. He got to his feet slowly. Then he started to rub his eyes.

"What's the matter?" asked Joe.

"I keep seeing double." Frank reached up and touched his forehead. "And what's this thing on my head?"

Joe looked up. "It's a bump," he told his brother. "You'd better get some ice on that."

Just then Biff returned with Spike Nolan, who was carrying an ice pack. "What happened here?" Nolan asked, staring at Frank.

"The batting machine went nuts," Joe said. "One of the balls hit Frank in the head. We tried to shut the machine off, but it was jammed. So we knocked it over. I think we broke it."

"Machines can be fixed," Nolan said. He reached out a hand and touched Frank's forehead gently, making him wince.

"It doesn't look too bad. But I don't like that swelling. You'd better have it checked out at the

23

hospital. Keep this ice pack on until you get there." He handed Frank the ice pack and left to examine his damaged pitching machine.

Joe and Biff came over to him. "What's wrong with it?" asked Joe.

Nolan shrugged and shook his head. "I don't get it. This machine is pretty reliable. It's never malfunctioned. Why is it acting up now? Come on, you guys, give me a hand lifting it back up again. I've got to find out why this happened."

Joe and Biff helped Nolan right the machine. After Nolan had examined it for a few minutes, he frowned and said, "I can't believe it. The feeding arm is bent. How could that happen?"

Joe inspected the machine. "Hey, look at this," he said suddenly. He reached inside and pulled out a piece of blue-and-white cloth that had been wedged into the speed controls. As he unfolded the cloth, he saw that it was a sweatband.

"That looks just like Tony's," said Biff as he peered over Joe's shoulder.

"Yeah, it does," Joe admitted. "But Tony's wearing his."

Just then, Tony walked up to them, smiled, and held out his hand. "Where'd you find my sweatband, Joe? I was looking all over for it."

"It was jammed in the machine," Biff said evenly. "I just don't understand you, Tony. First you rig the stands to collapse. Now you jam up the pitching machine. Why are you doing it? For laughs? Well, it's not funny."

"Take it easy, Biff," said Joe.

"No way, Joe. I hurt my hand yesterday. Today Frank gets beaned." He glared at Tony. "When is it going to stop?"

Tony glared back at Biff. "You know, I'm getting pretty tired of having to defend myself," he said. "What is it with you, Biff? Anytime something happens, you blame me. I don't have to take this." Tony started to walk away.

"Oh, no, you don't," yelled Biff. He sprang at Tony, wrestling him to the ground. Spike Nolan and Joe pulled them apart.

"Wait a minute," Joe said, stepping between Biff and Tony. "What are you guys fighting for, anyway?"

"Ask him," Tony said, pointing at Biff. "He started it."

"Knock it off, you guys," Frank said. "You're supposed to be friends, remember?" Suddenly, he clutched his head with both hands and began to weave back and forth. "I don't feel so good," he said. "I think I'd better get to the hospital."

Joe put his arm around Frank's shoulders to steady him. "Can you make it to the van?" he asked.

Frank nodded. The two of them walked slowly toward the parking lot. Biff gave Tony a final angry look and headed for the parking lot too.

"I'll phone the hospital and tell them you're on your way," Nolan called out.

Joe made sure Frank was sitting comfortably in the van, his seat belt buckled. Then he started the engine and drove to the hospital as quickly as he could.

An hour later, Joe was still sitting outside the emergency room of Bayport General Hospital waiting for the doctor's report on Frank's condition. Joe was just about to ask the nurse at the reception desk what was happening, when a harried-looking doctor stepped into the waiting area. "Is Joe Hardy here?" he asked.

Joe jumped up and approached the doctor. "I'm Joe Hardy," he said quickly. "Is my brother all right?"

The doctor smiled at Joe. "I'm Dr. Thaler, and your brother is going to be fine. He just has a mild concussion. We're going to keep him here overnight so we can observe him. It's very routine."

"Can I talk to him?" Joe asked.

"Sure you can. But only for a few minutes. He's in examination room four."

Joe found the room easily. When he stepped inside, he saw Frank lying on a hospital cot. He was pale but he was smiling.

"I called Mom and Aunt Gertrude," Joe told him. "They're on their way over. How are you feeling?"

"A little woozy, but okay," Frank replied. "You know, while I've been lying here, I started thinking about those two 'accidents' at camp." He raised himself up on his elbows slightly and looked at his brother. "It seems to me that somebody's going to a lot of trouble to frame Tony for them," he said.

"I know," Joe said, nodding. "Do you have any ideas on who that somebody might be?"

"Well, it can't be anybody from the Bombers," replied Frank. "That just doesn't make sense."

"What about Carter or Horner—or even Nolan? Could it be one of them?"

"It's possible. Unless it's an outside job." Frank let his head drop back gently onto the pillows. "As soon as I get out of here, we're going to do a little investigating," he said with a frown. "I don't like seeing my friends set up."

The next day was very hot and humid. The midday sun beat down on the baseball diamond. Frank was glad he was sitting in the shade of the center-field wall. As he watched outfield practice, he felt the knot on his forehead. It was the size of a Ping-Pong ball, and it still hurt when he touched it. He had been released from the hospital in the morning, and the doctor had told him to take it easy, so he wasn't practicing with the rest of the team.

It was almost time for the team's hour-long lunch break. Spike Nolan was using the time before lunch to hit pop-ups for the outfielders to catch.

Joe crouched in short center field, pounding his glove. "Okay, Mr. Nolan. I'm ready," he called.

Nolan crashed a towering fly ball deep into center field. It was over Joe's head, but he got a good jump on it and settled under the falling ball. It should have been an easy catch. But the ball tore through the webbing on his glove and bounced onto the outfield grass. Joe's mouth dropped open as he stared at his glove in astonishment.

"I can't believe I missed it," said Joe.

"What's the matter, Joe?" asked Tony with a laugh. "Got a hole in your glove?"

Joe looked at his glove, then at Tony. "That's exactly what I've got," he said, shaking his head. Biff and Frank walked over to them. Joe held his glove out. "Look at this. It fell apart, like a piece of junk. What's going on here?"

"Ask him," Biff said, jerking his thumb at Tony. "You just don't quit, do you, Prito?"

"Lay off, Biff," Frank said quietly.

"All I know is that every time he's around, something happens. It looks pretty suspicious to me," Biff replied.

"It sure does," agreed Dave Hoffman, a Bomber second baseman. "Someone greased the handle of my bat this morning. It slipped out of my hands during batting practice. And I saw Tony near the bat rack just before I went to hit."

"Yeah, I was near the bat rack," Tony said shortly. "I was up next. I was looking for a light bat."

"Sure you were," Dave said, with a smirk.

Tony pointed a finger angrily at him. "You'd better watch what you're saying. I don't like it."

"Then why don't you stop playing these dumb jokes?" Biff said hotly.

"Leave me alone, you guys. I didn't do anything. Why don't you believe me?" Without another word, Tony turned and walked off toward the parking lot.

Just then, Spike Nolan ran up to them. It took the overweight former catcher a minute to catch his breath, then he asked, "What's going on here?" He turned to Joe. "Why did you miss that easy fly?" he asked.

"How can I catch flies if my glove falls apart?" Joe gave the glove to Mr. Nolan. Then Dave Hoffman told him about the greased bat.

Nolan looked at Dave, then stared at the frayed webbing of Joe's glove. "Okay," he muttered. "Enough is enough." He handed Joe the glove and marched off in the direction of the dugout. The rest of the Bombers drifted off to have their lunch.

Frank and Joe looked at each other. They had both seen the anger on Spike's face. Frank nudged Joe. "Look, he's talking to Zeke Horner. Come on, let's eavesdrop."

They walked casually over to the dugout and pretended to look at some bats.

"I'm telling you for the last time, Horner, these accidents had better stop," they heard Nolan say angrily.

"Or what? Don't try to threaten me, pal. You can push these kids around, but not me. Remember that."

Nolan opened his mouth to reply, then snapped it shut. He gave Horner an angry look, turned, and left the dugout.

Joe glanced at Frank. "What was that all about?" he asked in a low voice.

"Let's find out," replied Frank.

The brothers stepped into the dugout and sat beside Horner on the bench. "Hi, Mr. Horner," Frank said. "How's it going?"

Horner didn't answer. He just stared straight ahead. Then he took a pink rubber ball from the pocket of his windbreaker and began to squeeze it with his left hand.

"What's the ball for?" Frank asked curiously.

"To keep my hand limber. A pitcher has to have strong fingers. By squeezing the ball I build up finger strength."

"We just happened to hear Mr. Nolan talking to you about the accidents and—"

Horner jerked his head toward Frank. "What are you doing, listening in on my conversations?" he snapped. "Get lost."

"Hey, you can't talk to my brother like that," Joe said hotly.

"I'll say anything I want. You're students at this camp. I'm an instructor. Keep your mouths shut and maybe you'll learn something." Horner stormed away.

Frank and Joe followed him out of the dugout. "All we want to know is what *you* know about these accidents," Frank called out.

"Are you deaf?" yelled Horner as he spun around. "Didn't you just hear me tell you two to get lost?" He glared at the brothers. Then he cocked his arm.

His release was so quick that the Hardys had

no time to react. The rubber ball was a blur as it left his hand.

Instinctively, Frank and Joe dropped to the ground. The ball, narrowly missing Joe's head, bounced once—and exploded with a loud *bang*. Chunks of grass and dirt shot high into the air.

4 In Hot Water

The Hardys lifted their heads and turned to look at the small crater left by the explosion. Little fires flared in the grass, but they were quickly blown out by the wind.

Joe and Frank got slowly to their feet. Horner was staring at the crater and muttering to himself. He was so shocked by the blast that he forgot Frank and Joe were there.

"If I'd really squeezed that doctored ball, I'd have lost my hand. Somebody's going to hear about this," he muttered.

He turned and walked unsteadily toward Spike Nolan's trailer, never once looking behind him. Frank and Joe followed him quietly. Horner tried to get into the office, but it was locked. "Open up, Nolan," he yelled as he pounded on the door. No one answered.

Next, Horner headed for the telephone booth at the corner of the parking lot. Fumbling in his pocket, he drew out some coins and jammed them into the slot. He punched in a number, then started yelling into the phone. Even though he was yelling, Frank and Joe were too far away to overhear.

"I'd really like to hear what he's saying," Joe said.

"So would I," Frank replied. "Come on, let's play some catch. Then we can get close enough to hear him."

Frank tossed Joe a baseball, which his brother managed to catch in the pocket of his glove, since the webbing was all torn away. They threw the ball back and forth, all the while edging closer to Horner. As they got nearer, Horner's voice became clearer. Finally, the brothers could hear every word of the one-sided conversation.

"That was a stupid thing to do," Horner was saying into the receiver. "Even if you get me out of the way, you'll still have to deal with Nolan. He knows everything. And if anything happens to me, he'll go to the cops."

Horner listened for a minute, then his face went red with rage. "Don't threaten me," he yelled. "You'll pay for this. I swear it. You'll pay." Horner slammed down the receiver and ran to his car. He sped out of the parking lot in a flurry of screeching tires.

"What do you make of that?" asked Joe.

"I'm not sure," Frank replied. "But it looks

like Horner could be the answer to the accidents in camp. Let's check out where that ball exploded. We might be able to come up with some clues."

They walked back to where the explosion had occurred. Joe bent down to examine the crater. "Look at this, Frank. It's not very deep—just a couple of inches."

"But it was big enough to put a message across to Horner. I just can't figure out why."

Frank crumbled a handful of dirt and examined it, trying to find pieces of the pink rubber ball. He came up empty. Joe didn't do any better. They looked up when they heard someone calling them.

"Oh, hi, Tony," Joe said. "What's up?"

"I brought over a pizza. Want some?"

"Sure, we'll be right there," Frank said.

Joe stood up. "We might as well have some lunch. It doesn't look like there's anything here."

The three friends sat on the grass and helped themselves to large slices of pizza. Nobody said anything. Tony looked from Frank to Joe. "How's the pizza?" he asked hesitantly.

"It's great," replied Joe.

Tony nodded, then turned to Frank. "How are you feeling?" he asked.

"I'm okay," replied Frank. "Thanks for the pizza, Tony." He stood up and started to walk away, but Tony jumped up and grabbed his arm.

"Look, Frank, you've got to believe me," Tony said, a note of desperation creeping into his

34

voice. "I didn't do anything to mess up that batting machine. It must have been an accident."

"I know you didn't do it, Tony," Frank said with a sigh. "But it wasn't an accident. Somebody did it deliberately."

Tony shook his head. "It wasn't me," he insisted. Then he said, "Whoever used my headband to jam the machine must have found it—or stolen it! That headband was supposed to bring me good luck. Some luck. I didn't even hit the ball yesterday, and now everyone thinks I caused the accidents."

"We're not accusing you," Joe put in. "We believe you."

"Yeah, well, nobody else does," Tony replied bitterly. "I don't know how my sweatband got stuck in that machine or how those other accidents happened. And that's the truth."

Frank and Joe both smiled at Tony. "Don't worry," Joe said. "We think we have a lead on who's really responsible."

"I'm glad to hear *that*," Tony replied with a relieved sigh. Before Frank could add anything to Joe's statement, Spike Nolan's voice rang out.

"All right, you guys," he yelled. "This is a baseball camp, not a day at the park. Lunch is over. Let's play some ball." He called for Team A to take the field. Team B, Joe's team, was at bat.

Hammer Carter was there, but Zeke Horner was nowhere to be found and no one knew where he was. Spike Nolan was annoyed but didn't make any comments. Instead, he took on Horner's pitching chores himself.

Horner returned a half hour later. He was nervous and irritable, and he yelled at the players whenever they made any mistakes.

When Horner took the mound, he promptly picked off anybody foolish enough to take any kind of a lead. He brushed back players with high pitches, sometimes aiming right for their heads. Joe nearly got hit twice. When he protested, the ex-big leaguer just laughed at him.

By four o'clock in the afternoon, Frank's head was beginning to throb. He had been trying to watch both Horner and Nolan for the last two hours, but it hadn't been easy. The pitcher was a bundle of nervous energy, and he was all over the field, yelling at students and arguing with Carter and Nolan.

Joe was still pretty annoyed by Horner's behavior on the mound, and he kept trying to confront him. But the pitcher just ignored him, making Joe even more irritated.

"Heads up, Frank," yelled Biff Hooper. The burly teenager stuck out his glove and snared the pop-up right in front of Frank. "You almost got hit." Biff tossed the ball to another kid.

"Hey, Biff," Frank said. "Do you have a minute?"

Biff saw the serious look in Frank's eyes and nodded. He called out to a player on the bench to take his place in the outfield. Then he said, "Okay, Frank, what's up?"

Frank steered Biff toward the bleachers so that they could talk in private. "Look, Biff, there are a lot of strange things going on at this camp. First

36

the stands fell down. Then I got beaned when the automatic pitcher went nuts."

"Not to mention the greased bat, and gloves falling apart when you catch a ball. And did you see the baseball that unraveled when Hammer hit it?"

"What!" exclaimed Frank. "When did that happen?"

"About thirty minutes ago," replied Biff. "The ball just came apart. It was very strange. I'll bet our pal Tony struck again."

Frank shook his head. "He didn't do it."

"How do you know?" pressed Biff.

"Look, Biff, we all grew up together. And we know each other pretty well. Tony wouldn't try to hurt anybody and you know it."

"But he's always kidding around. It has to be him."

"You're wrong, Biff. Joe and I are convinced that Tony is innocent. What will it take to make you believe it?"

"You're always looking for proof when you work on a case. So prove it to me. I'm all ears."

Frank sighed. "We don't have all the facts yet, but I'll tell you what we've found out so far. After Joe's glove fell apart, Nolan and Horner had an argument. Nolan warned Horner that the accidents in camp had better stop."

"No kidding?" asked Biff, his eyes wide.

"That's right. Joe and I tried to find out what was going on, but Horner wouldn't talk to us. Then he got mad and aimed a ball at us."

"Did he hit you?"

"No, he missed. And a good thing, too. When the ball hit the ground, it exploded."

"What? I didn't hear any explosion."

"It happened at lunchtime when everyone was gone. Anyway, it was a small explosion. But listen, Biff. There's too much going on here. Joe and I can't be everywhere at once. We need help."

"What do you want me to do?" Biff asked.

"Keep an eye on Nolan," replied Frank. "Follow him everywhere. Joe and I will watch Horner."

"What about Tony?" insisted Biff. "One of you should be keeping an eye on him too."

Frank realized that Biff would continue to suspect Tony as long as the accidents continued to happen. "We'll check him out too," he promised Biff.

"Okay, Frank," replied Biff. "You can trust me. I'll watch Nolan like a hawk."

"Thanks, Biff. I knew I could count on you." Frank looked at the field and saw that it was empty except for Joe, who was walking toward them tossing a ball in the air and catching it.

"Looks like we're the last ones left," Joe said. "Want to catch a few?"

"I can't," said Biff. "I have a date later. I want to clean up a little and get home."

"Don't look at me," Frank told his brother. "I just put myself back on the disabled list. My head hurts a little."

"Okay, okay," Joe said with a sigh. "I guess it's time to hit the showers."

In the locker room, Frank, who wasn't wearing his practice clothes, watched his brother wad his clothes into a ball and stuff them into his locker. The cramped locker was already filled to overflowing with T-shirts, sweatpants, gym trunks, socks, and extra pairs of spikes.

"How do you find anything in there?" asked Frank.

"It's easy," Joe replied cheerfully. "You've just got to know where to look."

Biff passed by on his way to the shower, his rubber thongs flip-flopping on the floor with every step he took. Joe grabbed a towel and followed him. Frank sat on a bench nearby and flipped through a baseball magazine.

Biff stepped into the shower and turned on the hot water. "Hey, Joe, want to make this into a steambath?"

"How do we do that?"

"Simple. We turn on five of the hot-water taps as far as they can go. In a few minutes, the whole room will be filled with steam."

"Won't we get burned?"

"No way. We stand in the corner under a shower that's running at normal temperature. It's great. When we're finished we just shut off the hot-water taps one at a time."

"Sounds great," Joe said. "Let me just get my bar of soap. I forgot it." He stepped out of the shower as Biff began to turn on the hot-water taps.

Joe was halfway to his locker when he suddenly heard Biff yelp in pain.

39

Joe and Frank rushed into the shower room. Through a blanket of steam, they saw Biff slumped in a corner, trying to shield his body with his hands. All six shower heads were on and scalding steam swirled around in the cramped space.

"Biff! What happened?" cried Joe.

"I slipped on some soap and twisted my ankle. I can't stand up."

Frank tried to rush into the shower but the scalding steam forced him back.

"You've got to do something, fast!" yelled Biff. "I'm getting burned."

Joe tossed him a towel. "Cover yourself with this, Biff. We'll get you out of there."

Joe reached and tried to turn off the nearest water spigot. The hot water stung his hands and arms. Wrapping a towel around his forearm and hands, he tried again.

The spigot turned. But instead of shutting off the water, the spigot came off in his hand!

5 Attack on Spike Nolan

"What do we do now?" Joe asked in a desperate voice.

"There has to be a shutoff valve around here somewhere," Frank said. "I'll take the back of the locker room. You take the front. Let's go!"

As the Hardys searched the steam-filled locker room, Frank stumbled into a bench and nearly fell, but kept his balance. Joe slipped in a puddle of water and hit the floor hard, landing on his shoulder. The pain made his arm go numb, but he gritted his teeth and got to his feet. His eyes scanned the room.

When he looked up, he barely made out two large valves, high on the wall above the sinks. "They're over here, Frank!" he called to his brother. He climbed up on one of the sinks and tried to turn the valve that had an *H* printed on it. It was stuck!

"Frank! I can't turn this valve!"

Frank climbed onto the sink, and together they tried to turn the valve. It was hard going at first, but when they heard Biff call out, "Hurry up, guys!" they gave it all they had.

Their combined strength made the difference. Slowly, the valve began to rotate. Joe shouted, "Hang on, Biff! We're turning off the water." In another minute they had turned the valve around as far as it would go.

Frank and Joe climbed down from the sink and hurried into the shower area. Biff was sitting in the corner. His arms and most of the exposed parts of his body were red, as though he had a mild sunburn. He was gasping for air, and had to wait for the steam to clear away before he could talk. Joe tossed him another towel.

"Thanks," Biff said. "I was really worried there for a minute."

"Can you walk?" asked Frank.

"I don't know. My ankle's pretty sore." With Joe's help, Biff stood up slowly and tried putting weight on his foot. "It hurts," he said through clenched teeth. "But maybe if I try walking, it will be okay."

Joe and Frank each grabbed Biff under his arms and led him slowly into the locker room.

"Thanks, guys," Biff said. "My ankle feels better now."

"You're pretty lucky. It could have been a lot worse," said Frank.

"This is really incredible," Biff said. "Now you can't even take a shower without wondering whether someone's going to play a practical joke on you. I hate to say it, but do you think Tony had anything to do with this?"

Before Frank or Joe could answer him, they heard Tony call out their names. He strolled into the locker room. "What's the matter with you guys? Didn't you hear me calling out there?" His eyes widened when he saw Biff limping. "What happened to you?"

"Somebody messed around with the temperature gauge on the hot water," Frank told him. "It was close to boiling when it came out. Biff almost got scalded."

Tony nodded. "Yeah, it happened to me too," he said. "I was in here just before you guys, and I burned myself badly. See?" He pulled his shirt out of his jeans and showed them a large red welt on his stomach. "But I thought it was just the shower I was using."

"No, it was all of them," said Joe.

"This camp is getting really weird," said Tony, shaking his head.

"You can add the word *creepy*, too," muttered Biff.

"Do any of you guys know which locker is Horner's?" Frank asked suddenly.

"It's number sixty-six," replied Biff. "It's right next to mine. Why?"

"I think we should have a look inside it," Frank said.

"That's a good idea," Joe said. "But he has a combination lock like the rest of us. How can we get his locker open without damaging it?"

Frank looked at Tony. "Remember that magic trick you used to do? The one where you escaped from chains that were fastened together with a combination lock?"

Tony grinned and nodded. "I remember. That was one of my favorites."

"Can you do it now?" asked Frank.

"With or without the chains?" kidded Tony. "Yeah, I can do it. But why do you want to check out Horner's locker?"

"He and Nolan had an argument today about the accidents in camp. Horner denied having anything to do with them."

"Why don't you believe him?" asked Tony.

"I just have a funny feeling about him. He acted really strange today, and somebody tried to hurt him."

"How?" asked Tony.

"Horner squeezes a ball to keep his pitching hand loose. Somebody put an explosive in the ball and it blew up," explained Joe.

"Did he get hurt?"

Frank shook his head. "No. He had thrown the ball away. But he was scared. He phoned someone, then he got really angry and stormed off to his car. We didn't hear the whole phone conversation, but I think it's time to learn a little more about Zeke Horner. Maybe we can spot something in his locker."

"What are you looking for?" asked Biff.

"Anything I can find," Frank replied.

The four of them approached Horner's locker. "I hope I'm not too rusty," Tony said. "I haven't done this trick in a while."

He knelt down and took hold of the lock. Frank, Joe, and Biff watched closely as he twisted the dial. After about five twists, the lock clicked open. Tony stood up and grinned at Biff and the Hardys.

"How did you do that?" Biff asked, staring at Tony in amazement.

"Well, magicians aren't supposed to reveal their secrets," replied Tony. "And it's kind of hard to explain. Basically, I 'felt' the combination with my fingers."

"I guess I owe you an apology, Tony," Biff said. "I'm sorry I was on your back before about the accidents."

"Forget it. Hey, aren't you going to open the locker?" he asked Frank and Joe.

Joe opened the door. Lying on a damp towel at the bottom of the locker were a screwdriver, a wrench, and a pair of pliers.

"Look at this stuff," Frank said. "The perfect tools for booby-trapping the showers."

"That does it," Joe said. "I'm going to find out what's going on around here." He marched toward the locker-room exit.

"Where are you going?" yelled Frank.

45

"To Spike Nolan for some answers."

"Not like that you're not," Frank said. "You'd better put some clothes on."

They all laughed, including Joe.

After Joe and Biff had gotten dressed, the four friends headed for Nolan's trailer. As they got closer, they heard loud voices. Someone shouted and a child's high, thin scream pierced the air.

Suddenly, the door of the trailer burst open and two men surged out, holding Spike Nolan between them. Nolan tried to resist, but one of them, a man with a white streak in his straight black hair, punched him in the jaw. Nolan slumped over, unconscious.

"Hey!" Joe shouted. "Let him go!"

The two men glanced at the four teens, then they hurried toward the parking lot, dragging a limp Spike Nolan behind them.

"Let's get them!" yelled Joe, racing forward. He tackled the man with the white-streaked hair. The man loosened his grip on Spike Nolan, then lost his balance as Joe swarmed all over him. The man quickly recovered and aimed a wicked punch at Joe's nose.

Joe ducked, and the punch flew over his right shoulder. Before Joe could react, the man kicked Joe's legs out from under him. Joe hit the ground hard.

Then Tony jumped on the man's back and hung on. As the man tossed Tony to the ground, he looked around for Spike Nolan. Nolan had come

46

to and was crawling away. Before the man could reach Nolan, Joe was on the man again, trying to wrestle him to the ground.

Meanwhile, the other man, who was heavyset, with a blond beard, had tried to make a run for it, with Biff and Frank in hot pursuit. Biff hadn't gone very far when he started limping badly. He stopped, then knelt down and rubbed his sore ankle. Frank continued the chase without him, quickly gaining on the older man.

The bearded man looked over his shoulder and saw that Frank was about to catch up to him. Reaching into his pocket, the man turned and pulled out a switchblade knife. He flicked it open and pointed it at Frank, who stopped dead in his tracks.

"Forget Nolan and these kids!" the bearded man yelled to his partner. "Let's get out of here!"

The man with the white-streaked hair delivered a powerful blow to the side of Joe's head. Then he grabbed Tony and flung him into Joe, knocking them both to the ground. Then he sprinted off to join his partner.

Joe was dazed, and he staggered as he tried to get to his feet. He kept on seeing double, and he shook his head to clear away the dizziness. Ahead of him, he could vaguely see the two men climbing into a silver-colored sports car. Seconds later, the car roared to life. With a loud screech, the car peeled out, leaving a dark trail of burnt rubber as its rear tires smoked.

Frank watched in horror. The car was speeding

47

right for his brother! "Get out of the way, Joe!" he yelled.

But Joe, stunned by the blow to his head, just stood there. The car bore down on him. Joe's mind told him to run. But his feet wouldn't listen. He was frozen on the spot!

6 Torched Trailer

"Look out!" Tony shouted, and rammed his shoulder into Joe's back, pushing him out of the way of the speeding car. The two of them tumbled to the ground.

The silver sports car roared by, narrowly missing both boys. Joe got to his knees and tried to get the license number, but it was smeared over with mud. The car sped out of the parking lot.

Tony helped Joe to his feet. "That was a close one," he said.

"It would have been all over if it hadn't been for you," Joe said to him. "Thanks, Tony. I owe you one."

"Forget it, Joe. You'd have done the same for me."

As Spike Nolan staggered to his feet, Joe and

Frank ran over to help him. Joe held out his arm, and Nolan steadied himself.

"Are you okay, Mr. Nolan?" asked Frank.

Nolan didn't reply. Instead, his eyes grew wide with fear. "Leigh," he whispered hoarsely. Then he shook his arm free and ran back to his trailer.

"What is it with that guy?" asked Biff, who was testing his ankle with a few careful steps.

"I don't know," Joe said. "But I heard a girl scream before."

"So did I," said Tony.

"Come on. Let's see what's going on," Frank said.

When the brothers, Biff, and Tony got to Nolan's trailer, the door was still open. They could hear muffled sobbing. They stepped inside. Spike Nolan was sitting on a chair, comforting a girl who looked to be about twelve years old.

"Is everything all right, Mr. Nolan?" Frank asked quietly.

Nolan looked up and smiled. "It is now. Thanks to you guys." He took a huge red handkerchief out of his pants pocket and handed it to the girl.

"Thanks, Daddy," the girl said, sniffling.

"This is my daughter, Leigh," Nolan told them. "She's visiting me for a couple of days before she goes back to boarding school."

"Hi, Leigh," Frank said gently. "Are you feeling better now?"

Leigh nodded. "That was pretty scary, though," she said.

"I'll bet it was," said Joe.

50

"Who were those men, Mr. Nolan?" asked Frank.

Nolan's face turned red. "That's none of your business. I've thanked you for your help. Now would you mind leaving my trailer?" Nolan stood up and tried to herd the Hardys, Biff, and Tony outside.

But Joe refused to move. "I'm not going anywhere, Mr. Nolan," he said stubbornly. "There have been too many weird things going on at your camp. First, the stands collapse. Next, the batting machine goes crazy and my brother gets hurt. Then the equipment is sabotaged. Baseballs unravel and gloves fall apart."

"So what?" snapped Nolan. "This is a baseball camp. All of that equipment gets used, sometimes it breaks down. It doesn't mean anything."

"Maybe not," replied Frank. "But there's enough evidence to prove that the accidents were done on purpose."

"What are you trying to say?" asked Nolan.

"Earlier today, when the webbing on Joe's glove fell apart, you went over to Zeke Horner and told him that the accidents had to stop. What did you mean by that, Mr. Nolan?"

"Zeke's in charge of the equipment. I just meant that he had better check it all out to prevent any more accidents."

"Then why did he tell you not to threaten him?" asked Frank. "That's a pretty strong reaction, considering all you meant was that he should check out the equipment."

51

Nolan shrugged. "He's temperamental. You know how pitchers get."

"He's not the only one who's temperamental," replied Frank. "Somebody booby-trapped Horner's exercise ball. It blew up."

"What?" Nolan looked surprised. "When did that happen?"

"Earlier today," Joe replied. "And right after that, we overheard Horner on the phone telling someone that if anything happened to him, you would go to the cops. What did he mean by that?"

"Why don't you ask him? I don't know what you're talking about, Hardy. Make your point, if you have one."

"There was another accident today," Frank said. "Someone rigged the showers in the locker room so that the hot water couldn't be turned off. Biff and Tony got burned."

Frank studied Nolan's face closely. He looked shocked and worried. But there was something else registered there too—fear. Frank was sure that Nolan knew what was going on. Now, if he could only make him talk.

Spike poured himself a glass of water from the sink. His hand shook slightly as he raised the glass to his lips.

Leigh Nolan looked at her father, her eyes full of fear. Then she shifted her gaze to Frank.

"How long has Horner been threatening you, Mr. Nolan?" Frank asked quietly.

"He never threatened me, but . . ." Nolan hesitated.

52

"But what?" pressed Frank.

"Leave him alone!" Leigh Nolan suddenly shouted at Frank. "Get out of our house! You don't belong here!"

Frank played his last card. "If you won't help us, we'll have to go to the police," he told Nolan. "I'm sure they'll be very interested in what's been going on around here. And this time, I don't think Chief Collig will put the blame on Tony."

Nolan gave a short laugh. "You can go to the cops, but remember, it's my word against yours. And no crime has been committed."

Frank leaned toward Nolan. "Mr. Nolan, we're not leaving here until we get some answers."

"Get out!" yelled Leigh hysterically. She picked up a baseball bat and waved it at Frank. "You leave my father alone, or you'll be sorry."

"You heard her," snapped Nolan as he took the bat from her hands. "Get out."

Frank shrugged his shoulders. "Okay, we'll leave. We're going to find out the truth—with your help or without it." He stepped out of the trailer; Joe, Biff, and Tony followed close behind.

Nolan slammed the door behind them.

"That was a waste of time," Joe said, as the four of them walked to the area of the parking lot where their cars were parked.

"No, it wasn't," Frank said. "I found out that Nolan's worried. And that he's afraid of Zeke Horner."

"Why doesn't Nolan want to call the police? You think he's hiding something?" asked Biff.

"He's hiding something, all right," Frank said.

53

"But I don't know what. The only thing I'm sure about is that Zeke Horner is the key to this mess."

"But how?" asked Joe. "And what's the connection between Horner and Nolan?"

"That might be tough to find out," admitted Frank. "Neither one of them is talking."

"You said before that someone tried to hurt Horner with a booby-trapped ball," said Tony. "Could that be Nolan?"

"It's possible," Joe said. "If he suspected Horner of causing the accidents in his camp, he'd have a motive. Besides, they just don't like each other."

"How do you know that?" asked Tony.

"Because of the way they were talking to each other after my glove fell apart. It was pretty obvious that they didn't get along."

"What about those two guys who tried to kidnap Nolan?" asked Tony. "What's their story?"

"Good question," Frank said. "Horner could have sent them. Maybe one of them was the person Horner was yelling at over the phone." He shook his head. "I don't know." He turned to his brother. "What do you think, Joe?"

"I think we should go home and get some rest. It's been a long day. Besides, I'm starving."

"Hey, Biff," Frank said suddenly. "I thought you had a date tonight."

"My date!" Biff exclaimed. "I forgot all about it! I'd better give her a call." He headed for the phone booth. "See you guys tomorrow," he shouted as he broke into a slow jog. "My ankle's feeling better already."

The Hardys headed for their van, Tony toward his car.

Suddenly, the three of them saw the silver sports car drive into the parking lot. It moved slowly, almost as though the driver were searching for something. Suddenly, the car speeded up. The man with white-streaked hair leaned out of the passenger window, holding a bottle with a burning rag stuck inside. He threw it at Spike Nolan's trailer.

"That's a Molotov cocktail!" Joe yelled to Frank.

The bottle shattered the window of the trailer, setting the curtains on fire and sending tongues of flame shooting high in the air!

7 Highway Holdup

"Call the fire department!" Frank yelled to Tony. Then he and Joe raced for the burning trailer. Smoke covered the area, and they couldn't see more than a few feet in front of them. Coughing, Frank and Joe were forced to retreat out of the cloud of black smoke. As they did, they collided with Biff.

"What are we going to do?" Biff cried. Then he, too, started coughing as the smoke-filled air hit his lungs.

They moved away from the widening cloud of smoke.

"We've got to get into that trailer," Joe gasped, inhaling the fresh air deeply.

Covering their mouths and noses with their baseball caps, the three of them took only small breaths as they felt for the door to the trailer. Joe found it first.

He rushed into the trailer. The smoke was so thick he could barely see. His eyes teared and he coughed violently.

"Get down on the floor," he heard Frank say. "Smoke rises, and there's more oxygen down there."

The brothers and Biff dropped to their knees and crawled forward. Suddenly Joe's hand touched something soft. A man's hand. "I've got Nolan!" he shouted.

He dragged the unconscious man through the swirling smoke toward the door. As he neared it, Biff and Tony rushed past him carrying a limp form. It was Leigh Nolan.

Joe looked around for Frank, but the thick smoke made it impossible for him to see more than a foot or two in any direction.

Once outside, Joe tried to lift Spike Nolan over his shoulder, but he was too weak. He took a deep breath and got a lungful of smoke. Then he started to feel dizzy, and his vision blurred. The more he coughed, the weaker he felt. If only I could rest, he thought dreamily. Just a few minutes of sleep. That's all I need. Then I'll be fine. He closed his eyes.

Strong hands grabbed Joe under the arms. He felt himself being lifted over someone's shoulder. Before he could voice a protest, he was away from the smoke. Joe coughed violently when fresh air filled his lungs.

Frank gently laid his brother on the grass, and

57

a firefighter placed an oxygen mask over Joe's face. Joe gulped the pure air hungrily. His dizziness started to fade. He looked to his right and saw Biff and Tony lying next to him, both wearing oxygen masks. To Joe's left lay Spike Nolan and his daughter. Both were unconscious, and a paramedic hovered over them.

"Are you okay?" asked a woman's voice. Joe looked up and saw a young firefighter with a soot-streaked face bending over him.

Joe nodded and removed his oxygen mask. "What about my brother and my friends?"

"They're fine," she told him. "They took in too much smoke. Just like you."

Joe jerked his head to the left. "What about Mr. Nolan and his daughter?"

"They're unconscious. Both have burns and bad cuts. What happened, anyway?"

"I'll ask the questions around here," said a familiar voice.

Joe looked past the firefighter and saw Chief Collig. Frank was standing next to him. "Suit yourself," replied the firefighter with a shrug. "You're going to be okay," she said to Joe. "Just take it easy." She jogged off to help the other firefighters, who were putting out the fire.

Chief Collig and Frank knelt beside Joe. The chief looked at the brothers. "What do you two know about this?" he asked.

"How did you get here so fast?" countered Joe. "The fire only just started."

"We were called fifteen minutes ago. We got

here as soon as we could. It's a heck of a mess. How did the fire start?"

"Someone threw a Molotov cocktail—" Frank began.

"Who?" interrupted Chief Collig abruptly.

"We don't know," Joe replied. "Earlier today, Frank and I saw two guys dragging Spike Nolan from his trailer. Biff and Tony are witnesses to that too. We tried to help him and managed to scare the two guys away. One of them had a switchblade, and they were driving a silver-colored sports car. I tried to get the plate number, but it was smeared with mud."

"Why didn't you call the police?" asked Chief Collig quietly.

"We wanted to get Nolan's story first," Frank admitted.

Chief Collig nodded grimly. "Did you get it?"

Joe shook his head. "Nolan kicked us out. We were just about to head for home, when the two men came back. One of them tossed the Molotov cocktail at the trailer—and the whole place went up. We pulled out Nolan and his daughter."

Just then, they saw Nolan and Leigh being carried on stretchers to a waiting ambulance. It quickly sped away, its siren blaring.

"Could you identify the men who attacked Nolan?" prodded Chief Collig.

"Sure," replied Frank.

"Good. Tomorrow I want you two, Biff, and Tony to come to the station house and look at some mug shots."

"Okay, Chief. But—"

"But nothing, Joe. Just take it easy. You did fine for an amateur. Now let the professionals take over." The chief stood up and spoke quietly to a uniformed police sergeant.

Joe tapped Biff on the shoulder. "You okay, Biff?"

Biff nodded but he didn't take the oxygen mask away from his face.

"I feel sick," moaned Tony.

Joe managed a grin. "I don't feel so good myself."

"Were we too late?" Biff asked anxiously.

"I hope not," replied Joe. "One of the firefighters said Nolan and Leigh were unconscious."

They stared at the trailer, which was now totally blackened with soot. The fire was out, but clouds of dense black smoke continued to pour out of the open door and broken windows. A wave of dizziness washed over Joe.

Reaching down, he replaced the oxygen mask over his face. Soon, he was breathing easily and the dizziness had passed.

"I'm going to do a little investigating," Frank said in a low voice so Chief Collig wouldn't hear him.

Joe nodded.

Frank walked toward the fire scene. He hadn't gone very far when he saw black skid marks heading toward the trailer. He bent down to examine them.

"Hey! What are you doing there?" Officer Meyers came running over to him.

"Looking for clues," said Frank.

"Since when are you a member of the Bayport Police Department, Frank? Just keep moving. The investigators are coming over here, and I don't want anyone disturbing the crime scene."

"I'm only trying to help," said Frank.

"Thanks, but no thanks. Besides, the chief will get really angry if you don't get away from here. Give me a break, will you, Frank?"

Frank held up his arms. "Okay, I'll stay out of your way."

On his way back to Joe, Frank saw something glittering in the sunlight. He bent down and picked up a gold tie clip with the letters *DS* in diamonds. He hurried over to his brother and handed him the tie clip. "Look at this, Joe."

Joe studied the tie clip, then gave it back to Frank. "Finally, a lead. Let's show it to Chief Collig," Frank suggested.

Joe stood up and took a deep breath. "That's better," he said with a grin. "I thought I was going to have to wear that oxygen mask forever!"

The Hardys walked over to Chief Collig.

"Chief, I found something that I think you'll want to see," said Frank. He showed the chief the tie clip.

Chief Collig was unimpressed. "It's a tie clasp. What about it?"

"I found it in the grass near some skid marks. Those skid marks had to have been made by the

61

silver sports car. So this tie clip must have been dropped by one of the guys in that car, probably the one who threw the firebomb."

"Maybe," Chief Collig said. "Bring it with you when you come down to the police station tomorrow. Now go on home and get some sleep."

"But I—" Frank began.

"Thanks for the help," interrupted Chief Collig. "But tomorrow, okay?" He walked off toward his squad car.

Frank shrugged his shoulders and pocketed the tie clasp. He and Joe walked back to Biff and Tony, who were sprawled on the infield grass. "You guys were really great back there," Joe said. "Thanks for helping out."

"Hey, no problem," said Tony, grinning. "I've always wanted to be a hero."

Biff looked at Tony and rolled his eyes. "But seriously, guys," he said to Frank and Joe, "we're just glad nobody was badly hurt. At least I *hope* the Nolans are okay."

"Maybe we should stop in at the hospital on our way home to see how Leigh and Mr. Nolan are doing," Frank suggested to his brother. "Do you know what hospital they're in?"

Joe nodded. "Bayport General. I saw the name on the side of the ambulance."

"Count me out," Biff said. "I've got to get home and call Jenny. My date, remember? I just hope she's the forgiving type."

"Count me out too," Tony said. "We heroes need our rest."

"Can you get home okay?" Frank asked.

"Sure. I can still drive," Biff said. He turned to look at Tony, who nodded. "I'm fine," he assured them.

"See you guys tomorrow," Joe said as he and Frank headed for the van.

Joe sat behind the wheel of the van and rubbed his eyes. They still stung from the smoke. He glanced at Frank, who was leaning back with his eyes closed. Joe rolled down the windows and drove slowly out of the parking lot.

As he adjusted his sideview mirror, Joe saw a flash of silver. "Wake up, Frank, they're back," he said.

"Who's back?" Frank asked, opening his eyes.

"The guys who torched Nolan's trailer. Can't you see them?"

Frank checked the mirror on his side. Then he leaned out the window and looked back, craning his neck. He didn't see anything. "Nobody's there, Joe," he said.

"But I saw them," Joe said. "Wait a minute." He stared into the sideview mirror, and his eyes widened. Staying just out of sight was a silver sports car. He tried to get a better look, but a red sedan pulled in behind him.

"I was right. They're behind us, trying to stay out of sight."

Frank crawled to the back of the van and peered out the rear window. "I see them. They're in back of that red sedan."

"They must be following us," Joe said.

"Maybe they want to get any witnesses out of the way. Let's lose them."

As the traffic thickened, Joe had a hard time keeping track of the silver car. Other cars kept pulling in behind him.

"We have to get off this road, or we'll never shake them," Frank said urgently.

"The parkway's about a quarter of a mile away," Joe said. "I'll get on that. Then I'll show those guys what this van can do."

When the car right behind them turned onto a side road, its place was taken by a huge diesel truck. The driver honked his horn, trying to panic Joe into speeding up. It didn't work. Joe kept up a steady pace.

When the van stopped for a red light, Frank again looked out the rear window. "It's gone," he called out to his brother.

Joe nodded and gave his brother the thumbs-up sign. Then he glanced out the side window, and his mouth went dry. The bearded man smiled at him from the passenger side of the silver sports car. Joe's eyes widened. The man was holding up a pink rubber ball, the same kind that had exploded on the baseball field earlier.

The man's smile broadened as he drew back his arm to throw the ball into the Hardys' van!

8 Hard Drive

At the same moment, the light turned green. Joe jammed his foot on the accelerator and peeled out, leaving a trail of burnt rubber behind him. In the back, Frank was thrown to the floor of the van. Joe looked in his sideview mirror. The silver car was taking out after him.

"What's going on?" Frank yelled from the rear of the van.

"Those guys were going to throw an explosive into the van. Now they're really on our tail. Hold on!" Joe made a sharp right turn onto the entrance to the parkway and the van fishtailed wildly. Steering into the dangerous skid, Joe straightened out the van and sighed with relief. He raced down the parkway, at the same time carefully watching the progress of the sports car behind him.

"There's a turnoff up ahead," Frank said as he crawled back to the passenger seat. "It leads to a Shopper's City. We'll lose them there."

Shopper's City was an enormous mall with three parking garages and a maze of entrances and exits. Shoppers frequently got lost trying to get in and out.

With a burst of speed, Joe put some distance between the van and the sports car.

"There it is!" Joe spun the steering wheel and got off the parkway. He turned into an entrance of Shopper's City marked Entrance Two-S.

"Let's hope these guys don't do their shopping here," Joe said as he steered the van up the narrow roadway to one of the parking garages. He glanced into the mirror. The sports car was following close behind.

The roar of the sports car's high-speed engine grew louder as the car drew closer. Joe zipped into the garage and up the ramp. As he careened around a corner, he lost sight of the sports car for a moment. He turned the corner and spotted the exit sign. He headed down the exit ramp and out of the garage. Then he drove out of the shopping center through Exit Three-N. He circled Shopper's City until he found another entrance. He drove into the parking garage, picked a spot in the first level by the wall, and stopped the van.

Frank and Joe held their breath and waited. Then they heard the sound of a car behind them. The brothers froze.

Joe sneaked a glance out the window and gave a loud sigh of relief. Frank leaned forward to see.

66

A huge station wagon with a large family inside eased into the space next to the van.

"Looks like we lost them," said Frank.

"For now," Joe replied. "I just hope they're looking for us on the other side of the shopping center." He started the engine and headed for the exit. There was no sign of the sports car as Joe eased the van back onto the parkway.

Frank looked at his watch. It was nearly seven o'clock. "Why don't we stop for a quick burger?" he suggested.

"Good idea," Joe said with a nod. "I'm starving."

The traffic on the parkway was heavy. Joe drove slowly in the right lane, checking his sideview mirror every few seconds. But the sports car was nowhere in sight.

The Burger Bonanza was packed with cars when the van pulled in. Joe and Frank saw some of their friends from baseball camp and waved to them. The Hardys ate quickly and returned to the van.

Back on the road, Joe drove slowly, keeping a careful watch in his sideview mirror to make sure they weren't being followed. They hadn't gone very far when an ambulance rushed by with its lights blinking and siren squealing.

Just ahead, a dark blue van lay on its side. The accident scene was closed off by red flares, and the Hardys could see someone being wheeled to the waiting ambulance. Joe gave a low whistle. "That looks like it was some accident," he said.

A uniformed police officer, waving a flare, kept

the traffic moving. Standing beside the officer was a man in a sports jacket. Joe and Frank recognized Detective Con Riley, their good friend on the Bayport police force.

Frank rolled down his window as they drove by. "What happened, Con?" he asked.

"Two vehicles got into an accident. Witnesses say the van was edged off the road by a gray or silver sports car. When the van crashed and turned over, the sports car kept on going."

Joe's stomach twisted into a knot. "Was anyone hurt?"

Con shook his head. "The driver of the van was wearing his seat belt. His van is pretty well totaled, though."

The horn of the car behind the Hardys' van honked angrily. Con Riley stepped to the left and yelled out, "Keep your shirt on, buddy. Or I'll give you a ticket for disturbing the peace!" He turned to Frank and Joe. "You guys better move on too."

Away from the scene of the accident, the traffic opened up, and Joe was able to move along at a good speed. Every once in a while he glanced in the rearview mirror. Nothing.

"Do you think our friends in the silver sports car ran that van off the road?" Joe asked.

"I'd say it's a good bet," replied Frank. "They probably thought it was our van. I wonder how long it will take them to find out it wasn't."

Night was beginning to fall as the Hardys headed toward the hospital. As they passed a deserted gas station, a car pulled out from behind one of the gas pumps. The car screeched toward the van.

Quickly picking up speed, the driver cut the distance between the two vehicles. Frank and Joe had just enough time to identify the silver sports car. An instant later, the sports car's high beams flashed on. Joe glanced in the side-view mirror. Nearly blinded, he almost lost control of the van.

As he struggled with the steering wheel, the sports car pulled up beside the van, nudging it closer and closer to the grassy shoulder of the road.

Joe floored the accelerator, and his burst of speed caught the other driver by surprise. Joe quickly widened the distance between the van and the sports car.

Just ahead, the road forked. Joe swung the van to the right and again increased his speed. The sports car stayed right behind him, rapidly drawing closer to the van. Then it bumped the rear of the van, causing it to swerve wildly. It took all of Joe's driving skill to regain control.

Suddenly a train whistle wailed in the distance.

"If I can only stay ahead of this guy for a few minutes more," Joe said, "we'll cross the tracks first and the train will block the sports car. What do you think, Frank?"

"Do it. But hurry. They're gaining on us."

Joe made a right turn and sped along a road that ran parallel to the railroad tracks. The sports car was close behind. Joe turned the wheel hard to the left and roared up a side road.

The sports car made the turn and nearly skidded out of control. Joe was at least thirty yards ahead and getting farther away as the driver leveled off the car.

Joe made a hard right, and the glare of the sports car's high beams disappeared. Another quick right and a sharp left found the van back on the road running parallel to the tracks.

Joe smiled. His plan was going to work.

The clanging of a railroad crossing light snapped Joe out of his thoughts. He made another fast left onto the road crossing the tracks. As the safety gate lowered, Joe gunned the accelerator. The van lurched across the tracks. In the distance the train whistle blasted a warning.

The van hit a track and skidded, but Joe steered into the skid and braked gradually. The van stopped, angled across the tracks. Its front tires rested on the railroad ties. The rear wheels lay in the gravel of the roadbed.

Joe stepped on the accelerator. His rear wheels spun but had no traction. The faster the wheels turned, the deeper they dug into the gravel.

"Come on, Joe!" Frank yelled. "What are you waiting for?"

"We're stuck!" cried Joe. "I can't get the van to move!"

All of a sudden, they could see a beam of light. It grew brighter and brighter as the train bore down on them.

Joe glanced in the sideview mirror—and saw

the glare of a pair of headlights racing toward them from the road behind.

The train whistle shrieked again. Frantically, Joe rocked the van back and forth to free it. But it was no use. They were trapped! And the speeding locomotive was heading straight for them!

9 Searching for Answers

Joe floored the accelerator.

"Don't do that," Frank said. "You'll only make it worse. Try rocking the van again."

"That didn't work before."

"Just try it! We don't have much time."

Joe threw the van into reverse, then shifted into forward gear. The rear wheels caught, and the van struggled to free itself but sank back into the gravel.

"Once more," urged Frank. "You almost had it."

Again the train whistle shrieked. And the cab of the van was bathed in the locomotive's light. "Here goes nothing," said Joe.

The van bucked like an untamed horse as Joe

rapidly shifted gears. Kicking up a shower of gravel, the rear wheels caught. The van leapt forward. Joe sped from the tracks just in time. The engine roared past, its whistle cutting the silent night air.

Joe leaned over the steering wheel and caught his breath. "That was close," he said as the train thundered by.

"Let's get out of here," Frank said.

By using back roads, Joe hoped to keep the sports car completely off their tail. His plan worked, but it was time-consuming, and they arrived at the hospital only ten minutes before the end of visiting hours.

The receptionist told them that Spike Nolan was in room 209, on the second floor.

At the elevator, they were stopped by a burly guard wearing a blue uniform. "Visiting hours are over," he said.

"Not quite," Frank said. "We still have ten minutes."

"There's someone we really have to see," Joe said urgently.

The guard looked at them. "Okay, okay," he said with a sigh. "You can go up."

Frank was silent as they rode up in the elevator. "What's the matter?" Joe asked his brother.

"I've been trying to figure out why someone would want to sabotage a baseball camp."

"To close it down," replied Joe promptly.

"That's what I think. But I don't know why. Got any ideas?"

Joe shook his head.

The doors opened, and they followed signs to room 209. Frank put his hands in his pockets and glanced at his brother. "Well, I have a few," he said.

"What are they?"

But before Frank could answer, a nurse came up to them. "Can I help you?" she asked.

"We're on our way to see Spike Nolan, in Room two-oh-nine," explained Joe.

The nurse shook her head. "I'm sorry, you can't see him tonight. He needs complete peace and quiet. But you can come back tomorrow." She smiled at them briefly and walked away.

Frank and Joe looked at each other. Joe shrugged. "Who wants to be a detective twenty-four hours a day, anyway? Let's go home."

They retraced their steps to the van. As they headed toward home, Joe asked, "So what are these ideas of yours?"

"Well, it's obvious Nolan is hiding something. Horner is too. Maybe it's something from both of their pasts."

"They were both professional baseball players, Frank."

"That's not what I mean. There must be something else. Don't forget what Horner said over the phone. Didn't he say that Nolan knew everything?"

"You're right. They have to be connected in some way. But how?"

Frank shook his head. "I don't know. We have to get Nolan and Horner to talk." Frank chewed

74

on his lower lip thoughtfully. "Then there are those guys in the silver sports car."

"I know," Joe said. "They acted like professional muscle. But why did they go after us?"

"We were witnesses to both of their attacks on Spike."

"So were Biff and Tony. How come they didn't go after them?"

"Maybe they did. We just didn't see it. Look, Joe, we have a reputation in this town. Those guys could have asked around and found out that we're detectives. They probably figured that with us out of the way, no one else would be able to stop them."

"It could also mean that whoever hired them lives in Bayport," Joe pointed out.

"That's also what I've been thinking," Frank replied, nodding. "But outside of that tie clasp I found, there are no other clues to help us identify either the muscle or who hired them." He looked at his brother. "But one thing is clear," he said. "Nolan's in big trouble. Whatever he's involved with, he's in way over his head."

"So what do you think it could be?"

"It could be anything. Gambling. Loansharking. Insurance fraud." Suddenly Frank's eyes lit up. "Wait a minute. A camp like Nolan's has to be covered by insurance, doesn't it?"

"Sure, but what does that have to do with anything?"

"Just listen a minute. Let's suppose that I open up a business. I finance this business by taking out a loan. Business is bad and I'm losing money,

75

but the loan still has to be paid. Otherwise I lose the business."

"So you fake an accident and hope that the insurance company will pay off. It sounds good, Frank."

"It gets better. Listen to this. Let's suppose that I couldn't get money from a bank or from relatives. Who would I get it from?"

"Loan sharks. They don't ask questions."

Frank smiled. "And how do they treat a slow payer?"

"They break his legs—or set his trailer on fire. Do you think the firebomb was a warning, Frank?"

"It could be. But the loan-shark theory doesn't cover a threat to Horner."

"What if it wasn't directed at Horner?" said Joe. "It could have been meant as a warning to Nolan to pay up or people would be hurt."

Frank shook his head. "I don't know, Joe. It doesn't fit together, somehow. We need more information."

"We need something else, too," Joe replied with a yawn. "Sleep!" He pulled into the driveway of the Hardy house and shut off the van's engine.

"Okay, okay," Frank said, laughing. "We'll call it a night."

The next morning, Frank was awakened by a phone call from Biff. "I got a call from Hammer Carter saying that camp was canceled today," Biff told him. "I said I'd call you with the news."

"Okay, thanks, Biff," Frank said sleepily. "What about tomorrow?"

"It's still on, as far as I know. You guys want to go to the beach today?"

"We can't," replied Frank. "We've got some investigating to do."

"Well, good luck," Biff said. "See you tomorrow." He hung up.

Frank replaced the receiver, turned over, and went back to sleep.

Two hours later, he felt someone shaking him.

"Frank!" Joe said. "We're late for camp. Two hours late, to be exact!"

Frank turned over and blinked at his brother. "Forget it," he said. He told Joe about Biff's call. Then he got out of bed. "Now we can go to the hospital earlier than we planned. And while we're there, I'll stop in and see the doctor who treated me for the concussion. He told me to drop by and get checked out."

"Don't forget we're supposed to stop by Chief Collig's office too," Joe reminded his brother.

"Right," Frank said.

After a breakfast of pancakes and sausages, accompanied by a lecture from Aunt Gertrude on the dangers of detective work, the Hardys set off for the hospital.

When they got there, Frank asked to see the doctor who had treated him.

"You're in luck," the nurse said with a smile. "Dr. Thaler can see you right now."

"Great!" said Frank. He stood up and started toward the examination room.

"Want me to go with you?" asked Joe.

"I'm sorry, sir, but you can't," the nurse said hastily.

"Don't worry, Joe," Frank said with a grin. "If I have a relapse, you'll be the first to know." He disappeared through the door of the examination room.

Joe picked up a magazine and leafed through it.

Fifteen minutes later, Frank returned. "How'd you make out?" asked Joe.

"I'm in perfect health," said Frank.

"Great!" shouted Joe. The nurse looked at him sternly and shook her head. "What about the headaches?" he asked in a quieter voice.

"The doctor said they were normal after being hit in the head. They'll disappear in a couple of days."

"I'm glad you're okay."

"Me, too," Frank said. "Come on, let's go visiting."

They took the stairs to the second floor. As they passed the nurses' station, they saw an orderly with white-streaked hair entering Spike Nolan's room.

Frank grabbed his brother's arm. "Joe!" he said in a low voice. "Isn't that—"

Joe interrupted. "The guy I had the fight with. The guy who torched Nolan's trailer. The guy who's been chasing us in a silver sports car. Yeah. Come on!"

The door to Nolan's room was closed, but they could hear the sound of muffled screams and breaking glass. Joe pushed the door open and ran inside. Frank followed close behind.

Spike Nolan was sitting up in bed, his face a mask of fear. His hands clutched the wrists of the man, who was trying to smother him with a pillow!

10 Face-to-Face with a Suspect

"Stop!" yelled Frank.

Startled, the attacker looked up. He hurled a food tray at Frank, scattering eggs and splashing hot tea all over the room. Frank ducked, and the tray sailed over his shoulder. The man tried to run away, but Spike Nolan grabbed his hospital coat.

As the man tried to wriggle free, Joe ran over and leapt on him, knocking him to the floor. They wrestled. Then the man tossed Joe away from his body easily.

"Go after him," yelled Nolan. "He's getting away."

Joe got to his feet quickly, but slipped on a pile of scrambled eggs. As he fell, the man grabbed him and aimed a punch at his jaw. Joe moved his head away in time, and the man struck the wall instead. Thrown off balance, he released his grip on Joe, who fell to the floor.

The man tried to run from the room, but Frank blocked his path. Frank moved closer to him. Suddenly, as Joe was about to jump him again, the man reached into his pants pocket and pulled out a switchblade knife. He flicked it open and pointed it at Frank. Joe froze.

"Stay right where you are," the man commanded.

Frank didn't move. "You won't get away with this," he said.

"Shut up, kid. You and your brother are sticking your noses into things that don't concern you. I ought to teach you both a lesson."

"Leave them alone," Nolan cried. "They've got nothing to do with this. It's me you want."

The man momentarily shifted his gaze to Nolan. Now's my chance, thought Frank. He hurled himself through the air, hitting the man across the legs. The knife skittered across the room as the two of them tumbled to the floor.

The man was bigger and stronger than Frank. After a few seconds of tussling, he managed to trap Frank in a stranglehold. Then he looked up. Joe was rushing headfirst toward him. The man released Frank, ripped down the courtesy curtain, and tossed it over both brothers.

While the Hardys struggled to get out from under the curtain, the man bent down and retrieved his knife. Then he yanked the door open and ran out of the room.

"He's getting away!" Nolan yelled.

The Hardys finally managed to untangle themselves from the curtain. They hurried over to Nolan to see if he was all right.

Nolan was a sorry sight. His i.v. tube had been pulled from its plastic squeeze bottle, and it trailed beside him. The back of Nolan's hospital pajamas had loosened and his polka-dot underwear was showing.

"Don't worry about me," Nolan said. "Get that guy!"

Frank stayed with Nolan while Joe took off in pursuit of the man. He saw a white coat trailing from the staircase door. Joe raced for the stairs.

In the stairwell, he could hear the man breathing heavily, and Joe knew he was tiring. I'll get him now, he thought.

At the base of the stairs, Joe got a good look at the man he was following. And found that he had been chasing the wrong guy. A gray-haired doctor looked up at him in surprise.

"Do you want me?" he asked.

"Did you see an orderly with a white streak in his hair come down these stairs?"

"No. Maybe he used the elevator."

Now I'll never get him, Joe thought and ran past the doctor to the stairway exit. The lobby was crowded with people. Joe scanned the bustling reception area, but the man with the white-streaked hair was nowhere to be found.

Joe ran to the bank of elevators. He stopped in front of a thin-faced security guard.

"Did you see an orderly with white-streaked hair come by here?" Joe asked.

"Sure did. He ran into the parking lot just a few minutes ago."

Joe darted outside. Running between the rows of parked cars, he scanned the area. On the ground in front of him lay a soiled lab coat. He checked the pockets but they were empty. He's got to be around here somewhere, he thought.

A car started up two rows away. Before Joe could react, a silver sports car sped away, narrowly missing a station wagon that was trying to park.

Joe watched helplessly as the car vanished in the distance. He returned to the lobby and rode the elevator back to the second floor. A crowd of people had gathered outside Nolan's room. He could hear Nolan yelling.

Joe elbowed his way through the crowd. "I'm okay," Nolan was saying. "Will you stop fussing over me like I'm a baby?"

A stern-faced nurse stood over him. "You get back into this bed, Mr. Nolan. Now."

Nolan hesitated but the nurse was not about to be intimidated.

"If you don't get back into your bed I'll call an orderly and he'll put you there."

Nolan sat on his bed. "You can't talk to me that way," he said.

"I'll talk to you any way I please. You're a

patient here." She reconnected his i.v. tube as she spoke. "You have to follow our rules. Just look at this room. It's a mess. What were you doing in here?"

"I was having a nightmare," said Nolan.

The nurse raised her eyebrows. "You can do better than that," she said.

"No, it's true," said Frank.

The nurse turned to Frank. "And who are you?" she asked in an icy voice.

"I'm Frank Hardy. I was down here just sitting by Mr. Nolan's bed. He was asleep and suddenly he started thrashing around. Before I could stop him he had knocked over the water pitcher and tray."

"Why didn't you call for a nurse? All you had to do was press this button." She held up the call button. "Someone would have been here in a minute."

Frank lowered his head and tried to look sheepish. "I guess I just panicked. I'm sorry."

The nurse was not finished. "It could have been serious," she said sternly. "Mr. Nolan could have been having a seizure or a heart attack. Use the button next time."

Turning to Nolan, the nurse said, "You'll have to get out of bed for a few minutes while I have an orderly clean it up. I'll help you into the wheelchair."

"I'll do it," offered Frank, and wheeled the chair over to the bed. With Joe's help, he eased Nolan into the chair and pushed him to the window.

84

"What happened to our friend with the knife?" Frank asked his brother.

"He got away," Joe said.

"We have to talk, Mr. Nolan," Frank said.

"I've got nothing to say," Nolan said.

Frank wheeled the chair out of the room into the corridor. In the harsh light, he could see the bruises on Nolan's face and the burns that covered the backs of his hands.

Nolan wouldn't look at Frank. "Leave me alone, kid," he said quietly. "This is none of your business."

Frank turned the chair around and crouched down until he was face-to-face with Nolan. "You listen to me, Mr. Nolan. When my life is threatened, then it *is* my business. Someone tried to kill me with that pitching machine."

Nolan grunted. "You've got some imagination, kid. That machine's pretty harmless. All it did was throw a couple of baseballs at you."

"I got hit in the head."

"You should have been wearing a batting helmet. You know the rules."

"Are you saying that it was an accident?" asked Joe.

"Sure it was. Remember the waiver you signed when you started camp? We're not responsible for any injuries suffered by any of the students."

"What about the faulty equipment?"

"We purchased a bum lot. It can happen to anyone."

"What about the defective shower spigots?" Frank asked.

"Those aren't mine. They belong to the town of Bayport. You'd better tell the board of education to check the maintenance schedule at your high school. The showers could use some servicing."

Joe shook his head. "You're something, Mr. Nolan."

"If you're finished," Nolan said, "I'd like to get some sleep." He rolled the wheels with his hands and headed back to his room. Frank watched him go.

"Hey, Mr. Nolan. Maybe next time that guy won't be so clumsy," said Frank.

The wheelchair stopped.

"What guy?" Nolan said with a shrug. "I was having a nightmare. You said so yourself."

Joe called out, "Did that nightmare drag you into the parking lot, Mr. Nolan? And did it toss that Molotov cocktail at your trailer?"

"I can take care of myself, kid. Don't you worry about me. Worry about yourself."

Frank and Joe walked over to him.

"What about your daughter?" Frank asked. "Next time maybe they'll skip you and go after *her*."

"Just leave my daughter out of this," Nolan snapped.

"She could have been hurt, Mr. Nolan. Don't you think you should go to the police?"

"What for? They can't help me."

"Maybe they can't," Joe said. "But we can."

"You're just kids. What do you know?"

"We know that a man doesn't get threatened

86

for no reason," Joe said. "Listen, my brother and I have done detective work before. We'll keep it confidential if that's what you want. But if a crime has been committed, then we'll have to go to the police."

"I don't want the cops involved in this," Nolan said.

"Why not?" asked Frank.

"I've got my reasons. Anyway, why should I trust you?"

"Look, you say you don't want the police involved," Frank said. "But they're already investigating the firebombing of your trailer. Eventually, Collig will find out who those guys are and what they're up to. But the police can't work full-time on this. We can. And the faster we solve this case and nail whoever's responsible, the better it'll be for you and your camp."

Nolan sighed. "Maybe you're right. I've got to talk to someone. Maybe all this will finally end." He looked at Frank and Joe. "I know who's been causing those accidents in camp."

11 Spike Nolan's Story

Frank stared at Nolan. "Who is it?" he asked.

"It's Zeke Horner," said Nolan.

"Why haven't you done something about it?" asked Joe.

Nolan looked at him, a pained expression on his face. "You just don't understand."

"We're listening, Mr. Nolan. Why don't you explain it to us?" said Frank encouragingly.

Nolan put the brake on the wheelchair and faced Frank. His eyes had a haunted look, and sweat beaded on his forehead. He wiped it away with the back of his hand. "Horner has been blackmailing me."

"Why?"

Nolan hesitated, then shrugged his shoulders.

"It started a long time ago. I was twenty-one. Just a kid. And I made the big leagues. It was a dream come true and I had to keep pinching myself to make sure it was real."

"Go on," urged Frank.

"Rookies didn't play then. They rode the bench until one of the starters couldn't do the job anymore."

"How did you meet Horner?"

"He was our star pitcher. He was really something! He won twenty-nine games that year. And five of them were no-hitters. I idolized him. Did everything for him. Picked up his dry cleaning. Ran errands for him."

"What happened?" asked Joe.

"One day, the clubhouse man told Horner there was a package outside for him. Horner asked me to go out and get it. A messenger gave me a plain white envelope and I took it. All of a sudden, there were cops all over the place. They pulled guns and slapped handcuffs on me."

"What for?" asked Frank.

"The envelope contained fifteen thousand dollars. I had never seen so much money in one place before. I didn't know where it came from. The cops didn't believe me. They accused me of taking bribes."

"Did you?" asked Frank quietly.

"I never took a bribe in my life. But, as I said, the cops didn't believe me. They locked me up. The team bailed me out, but it wasn't the same after that. Nobody would talk to me, and the players stayed away from me like I had some kind of disease." Nolan's face sagged.

"What happened then?" asked Frank.

"I wanted to clear my name. But it was no use. The baseball commissioner accused me of accepting bribes from gamblers, and he kicked me out of baseball. I was blacklisted. Every major-league team knew what had happened. I never played with any of them again."

"I never heard anything about that," said Frank.

"You wouldn't have. They kept it pretty quiet. Didn't want to ruin the integrity of the game with a lot of bad publicity."

"But how could they keep it out of the papers?"

"It wasn't out of the papers," Nolan said. "They just reported a different story than what really happened. And besides, I was only a rookie. No one cared."

"So Horner was taking bribes," Frank said slowly.

Nolan laughed bitterly. "You got it. When I got out on bail, I went to him and told him that I would tell the commissioner everything."

"What did he do?"

"He broke down and cried. Told me that he needed money real bad to pay for an operation for his mother. He said he was so desperate for money that he started gambling. At first he won, but later he began to lose heavily. When he couldn't pay, he was threatened by the gamblers. They wanted him to throw a game or they would hurt him. When he refused, they changed their approach. They offered to pay for his mother's operation if he would help them."

"Why didn't you tell the commissioner?" Frank wanted to know.

"I couldn't. Even though I knew my playing days would be over if I wasn't cleared, I couldn't turn him in. He was everything I wanted to be in a baseball player. And I felt sorry for him. Why ruin his career for a moment of weakness?"

"What about your career?" Joe said quietly.

Nolan laughed. "I was a bench jockey, kid. An average catcher, a lousy pinch hitter, and I ran the bases like I had lead in my shoes. The team was planning to send me back down to the minors. I had nothing to lose. So I gave Horner a break and kept my mouth shut. The incident blew over quickly, and I was a forgotten man."

"What did you do then?" Frank asked.

"I still loved baseball. It was very important to me, so I opened up my camp. I kept in touch with Hammer Carter, the only player on the team who would still talk to me. When he retired, I hired him as an instructor. The two of us did okay in the beginning.

"But the camp didn't really get going until I took it on the road. I started raking in the bucks. I did real well until Zeke Horner showed up."

"Why did he come to you?" asked Joe. "You'd think that he'd stay away after what he did to you."

"By that time, he'd retired from baseball. Anyway, one day he showed up at a camp we held in Virginia. He was broke and scared silly. He told me he needed money to pay off some gambling debts."

"He was still gambling? Hadn't he learned his lesson?" Frank broke in.

"Guess not. He was in bad shape. He had a three-day-old beard, and he needed a bath. I told him to get lost. He told me that some men were looking for him. I didn't want to listen to him, so I tried to walk away, but he grabbed my arm.

"Then he got real quiet. He told me that if I didn't help him, he'd tell the newspapers the 'truth'—that I was kicked out of baseball for gambling."

"You should have gone to the police."

"Are you crazy? I didn't want that kind of publicity. It would have shut my camp down in a minute. My wife had recently died, and I had a kid to support. How was I going to do that if I didn't have a business? I gave him some money, hoping he'd go away."

"But he didn't," Frank said.

"You got that right. He just kept on hitting me for more money. I put him on the payroll, but it didn't do any good. He's had so many advances on his salary that he should be working the next five years for free. Finally, I couldn't take any more. I told him no more money. Then the 'accidents' started."

Frank looked at Spike Nolan. "You could have gotten killed today," he said.

"I know. I was just lucky."

"But how long do you think your luck is going to hold out?"

"As long as it has to," Nolan said stubbornly.

"What about those guys at your trailer? What do they have to do with all of this?" Joe asked.

"I don't know," Nolan replied, shaking his head. "Horner's been real jumpy lately. Maybe he's changed the rules now."

"What rules?"

"Whenever Horner would threaten me, there would be some little accident at the camp. Like bats breaking when you hit a ball. Or baseballs that would unravel when they were hit. Little things to let me know that he could do real damage if he wanted to. I can't figure out why he sent those goons after me. Unless he's trying to tell me that he's through playing around."

"Maybe Horner didn't send them," Frank said thoughtfully.

"Then who did?"

"What if gamblers were after Horner to pay up? He'd promise them anything just to keep them away from him."

"But what does that have to do with me?"

"Horner could have told them you were the problem. Preventing him from getting the money to pay them off. That would make them mad. You'd become a target."

"Horner has been trouble for me from the moment I met him." Nolan made a fist and pounded on the armrest of the wheelchair. "He got me kicked out of baseball. Now he's trying to

93

implicate me in whatever new dirty business he's involved in."

"You've been lucky, Mr. Nolan," Frank said. "Someone's tried to kill you twice and failed. And chances are he'll try again. Don't you think it's time you got some help on this?"

Nolan looked thoughtful. "What do you suggest I do, Hardy?"

"Let my brother and me handle this case."

Nolan considered the offer, then smiled. "Okay, kid, you've got yourself a deal. But remember, I don't want my past becoming public knowledge. Can you do it?"

Frank nodded. "We can try. But you have to trust us."

Nolan grunted. "The last time someone asked me to trust him, I was kicked out of baseball." He sighed. "I can hardly wait to see what'll happen now."

12 Batter's Choice

The next day, camp went on as usual except for the absence of Spike Nolan. His sessions were divided between Hammer Carter and Zeke Horner.

Near the end of the day, Joe was standing in the infield. He settled under a pop-up and pounded his glove—but instead of catching the ball, he let it glance off the heel of his glove. It skipped into the outfield.

"What's up, Joe?" yelled Carter. "You haven't caught anything today."

"Sorry, Coach, I guess I'm just not concentrating."

"Then why don't you call it a day? You're not doing any good here. Camp is over in half an hour, anyway."

"Good idea," said Joe. He jogged off the field and looked for his brother.

He found Frank sitting on the grass, watching the other pitchers warm up. Frank smiled. "How's it going, Joe?" he asked.

"Lousy. I can't concentrate."

"Neither can I. I've been thinking about this case all day. We've got to find out who owns that tie clasp."

"I know," Joe said, nodding. "And who our friends with the white-streaked hair and the blond beard are."

After the Hardys had left the hospital the day before, they had gone to the police station and looked at three books full of mug shots. They hadn't recognized any of the faces. And they hadn't seen Chief Collig to give him the gold tie clasp. He'd been called down to City Hall on another case before they got to the police station.

"And most important," Frank said now, "we've got to get Horner to talk."

"So why don't we go talk to *him?*" suggested Joe.

The brothers found Zeke Horner loading baseballs into the pitching machine.

"Mind if we ask you a couple of questions?" asked Joe.

"Forget it, Hardy," Horner said. "I told you once already to leave me alone."

"But—" Suddenly Joe was interrupted by Frank.

"Hey, Mr. Horner," Frank said. "How's your fastball today?"

"A lot faster than you'll ever hit."

"Want to make a bet?"

Horner chuckled. "What's the bet?"

"Just this," Frank said. "I'll bet that I can hit at least one pitch out of three you throw me."

"You're crazy. I'll strike you out."

"I guess that's something we'll have to find out."

"What are the stakes?"

"I get a hit, you tell me everything you know about the accidents in camp and those guys who firebombed Mr. Nolan's trailer."

"What if you lose?"

"Then my brother and I leave you alone."

"That's not much of a bet. I don't have to talk to you two at all."

"Better us than the police," Joe said. "They'd be very interested to know that you're blackmailing Mr. Nolan."

Horner's face went pale. He rubbed his mouth with the back of his hand. "I don't know what you're talking about," he said.

"Never mind," Frank said. "Is it a bet?"

"Sure," replied Horner, looking at Frank warily. "Let's get this over with."

Frank grabbed a bat and batting helmet. He readied himself in the batter's box as Joe crouched behind the plate.

Horner kicked at the mound, digging a pitching groove by the rubber. "You ready?" he asked.

"Let's go," said Frank.

The first pitch came in high and tight on the inside corner of the strike zone. Thinking the pitch would hit him, Frank dropped to the ground.

Joe helped him to his feet. He glared at Horner. "Watch those pitches," yelled Joe.

"It wasn't even close. Still think you can hit one?"

Frank nodded. "Throw me something to hit. I'll show you what I can do."

The second pitch was a scorcher that Frank couldn't even see. He swung wildly and missed the ball.

Horner didn't give Frank time to set up. He threw the third pitch sidearm.

Suspecting a trick, Frank swung early and hit the ball cleanly, sending it screaming right at Horner. The pitcher couldn't get his glove up fast enough, and the ball whizzed by him, bouncing into center field.

"Lucky shot," muttered Horner as he kicked at the mound.

Frank and Joe walked to the mound. "Okay, let's stop playing games," Frank said. "We know all about your blackmail scheme against Nolan. And we know that you caused all the accidents in camp."

Horner laughed. "So Nolan couldn't keep his mouth shut, huh?"

"Blackmail is a crime," Frank said. "The police will be very interested to know that when Nolan refused to pay you blackmail money, accidents began to happen in the camp."

Horner jabbed his finger at Frank's chest. "I'd watch what I was saying if I were you."

"Are you threatening me?" asked Frank.

"I don't make threats. Only promises."

"It looks like someone is making threats to you. Threats that might turn into promises."

"What are you talking about?"

"You could have lost your hand when that ball exploded. That was no accident. It seems to me that you'd jump at the chance to tell someone else what's going on. Unless you want to wait for the next exploding ball."

"Why don't you run along before you get hurt," Horner said.

Joe jumped in. "We're wasting our time here, Frank. Nolan said he'd make a statement. Let's go to the police." Joe grabbed his brother's arm and they walked away.

"Dumb move," whispered Frank as they got out of earshot. "What if he calls your bluff?"

"I wanted to shake him up," Joe replied. "He'll talk."

"I hope so," said Frank.

"Wait!" Horner called.

"I told you," whispered Joe.

Horner ran up to them with a look of panic on his face. "Can't we talk about this?" he asked.

"That's what we came here for, until you started making threats."

"Well, I'm not making threats now. When can we talk?"

"How about now?" Joe said.

"Forget it. Too many ears here. How about meeting me in my motel?"

"When?" demanded Frank.

99

"Six o'clock. It's the Bayview Motel on Cliff Road. Room twelve."

Frank nodded. "We'll see you then."

The Hardys turned and walked off toward their van. Joe leaned against the door and looked at his watch. "We've got three hours until six. What do you want to do now?"

Frank tossed his brother the diamond-initialed tie clasp. "It's a good thing Collig let us hold on to this. Now we're going to do some investigating. Last night, I made a list of all the jewelers in Bayport. Let's see if anyone remembers who bought this tie clip."

"It's a long shot," said Joe.

"What do we have to lose? It's a lead. Let's follow it up. We'll hit the Diamond Emporium first. It's in the Bayport Mall."

When they got to the mall, Frank parked near the entrance to the jewelry store. They entered the glitzy store, and a short salesman with glasses and a poorly fitting hairpiece rushed over to them.

"Let me guess," he said. "You're looking to impress your girlfriend, and you want to get her something personal. Right?"

"Not exactly," replied Joe.

"And you don't want to break the bank account," continued the salesman. "I've got just the thing for you." He pulled Joe by the arm and led him to a display case filled with gaudy ID bracelets.

Joe shook his head. "We don't want to buy

anything. We just want to ask you a few questions."

"I should have known. Go on, get out of here. I don't like comparison shoppers. When you know what you want, come back. If you don't, do me a favor. Stay home."

Frank held out the tie clasp. "We want to know if this was bought in your store."

The man looked at the clasp. "It might have been. What about it?"

"Look, we found this and we'd like to return it to the owner. Do you keep records of your sales?"

"Sure I keep records, but they're confidential."

"Can't you give us a break?" asked Joe.

"What's in it for me?" the salesman asked with a frown. "I'm pushing merchandise, not information."

Frank sighed. "Will you help us if we buy something from you?"

The salesman smiled a little. "I'm not promising anything, but my tongue gets awfully loose when my cash register is full."

"That's extortion," sputtered Joe.

"I prefer to call it aggressive salesmanship. Now what do you say?"

"How much for that money clip?" asked Frank.

"It's thirty dollars."

"I'll take it. Now, what about the tie clasp?"

The salesman studied the tie clasp carefully. "Yeah, this is mine," he said. "I sold a bunch of them two months ago."

"Can you tell us where to find the owner?" Joe asked him.

"Sure. I'll be just a minute." The salesman disappeared into the stockroom.

A few minutes later, he was back. "It was bought by a D. Sandler," the salesman reported. "He didn't leave his address."

"Do you remember what he looked like?" asked Frank.

"Are you kidding? I get at least fifty customers a day in here. The minute they leave I forget them. That's why I keep records. You got any complaints with my merchandise, you bring it back with the receipt within three days or it's yours forever."

He wrapped up Frank's money clip. Frank paid him, and the Hardys left the store.

Back in the van, Joe was furious. "I wouldn't have given that crook anything."

"But we got information we needed."

"All we have is a name. And no address. There could be dozens of people with the name *D. Sandler.*"

"Then we'd better start checking them out," said Frank.

As the van sped along, both brothers were quiet for a few minutes. Frank broke the silence. "Stop the van, Joe. Quick!"

Joe slammed on the brakes and the van skidded to a halt. "What's the matter?"

"I just saw the silver sports car."

"Where?"

"At the diner we just passed."

Joe made a U-turn, and they drove back to the diner. In the parking lot, Frank pointed out the silver sports car. Joe pulled into the empty space next to it, and the brothers jumped out of the van.

Inside the diner, Frank and Joe scanned the crowded room. They both saw their quarry at the same time.

Coming toward them was the man with the streaked hair. He was carrying a bag of food. His jaw dropped and his eyes opened wide when he spotted the Hardys.

"Hold it!" the brothers yelled in unison, and ran toward him.

The man dropped the bag of food and headed for the door. Joe changed direction and threw himself right in the man's path.

"Wait a minute," Joe said, holding up his hand. "You're not going anywhere."

"Want to bet?" replied the man. He pulled a pistol out of his jacket and pointed it directly at Joe.

"You're history," he said, and squeezed the trigger.

13 The Search for Sandler

Joe threw himself down, and the bullet whizzed past his ear, shattering the glass door. A woman screamed. The gun fired again. The man with the white-streaked hair raced by Joe and bolted from the diner. No one followed him.

Frank hurried over to his brother. "Are you okay?" he asked anxiously.

Joe nodded. "He missed me. I don't know how."

Joe stood up and brushed himself off, then walked over to an empty booth and sat down. Frank grabbed a glass of water and handed it to his brother.

Joe drank it down. Then he jumped to his feet. "What are we sitting around here for?" he asked. "Let's go after that guy."

The Hardys rushed to the door but ran into two uniformed police officers. "And where do you think you're going?" asked one of them.

"We're chasing after the guy who tried to shoot us," Joe said quickly. "Would you let us—"

"Settle down, guys. No one is going anywhere. The chief is on his way, and there are a lot of questions that need to be answered. Just take it easy and let us do our job."

"But—" Joe began.

"There are no buts. Sit down and be quiet."

"I don't believe this," Joe said angrily as Frank pushed him back into the empty booth. "That guy is getting away and we're stuck here with the police."

"Forget it, Joe," Frank said. "He's long gone by now anyway."

Chief Collig walked into the diner. When he saw Joe and Frank Hardy he rolled his eyes and shook his head. He stood in front of their booth.

"I should have known that you two would be involved in this," he said.

"We're ready to give our statement, Chief," said Frank. "But we've got somewhere to go. Could we please take care of this fast?"

"What's your hurry?" asked the chief. "Relax. You can talk to one of my officers in a few minutes."

The chief spoke to the owner of the diner.

Soon he had out a notepad and was jotting down information as fast as it was given to him.

Joe Hardy came over to him. "Since you're taking statements, Chief, how about taking ours?"

"In a minute. Just take it easy."

"Take it easy? Some guy just tried to shoot me. Look what he did to that door."

"I see what he did. But how do you know he was shooting at you? The waitress at the counter says the gunman was shooting at her. Look at that bullet hole in the mirror."

Joe turned around. The mirrored wall behind the counter had spiderweb cracks running from a circular hole in its lower left-hand corner.

"But, Chief," Joe said, "the guy was looking right at me when he fired."

"How come he didn't hit you?"

"He's a lousy shot," replied Joe.

The chief laughed. "Interesting theory, but it doesn't hold up. The owner says the gunman was only a few feet from you when he fired. At that range it's almost impossible to miss. He probably just wanted to frighten you."

"He did a pretty good job. Will you take my statement?"

"Save it for the officer, Joe. He'll be with you in a minute. Now, if you'll excuse me?" Without waiting for a reply, the chief walked away.

Joe rejoined his brother. "What are we going to do now? Just sit here and wait?"

"I don't know about you, but I'm going to

check the phone book and see how many D. Sandlers there are."

Frank returned a few minutes later.

"That was quick," Joe said. "How many did you find?"

"Just three."

"What? That's great. Let me see." He took the list from his brother's hand and looked it over.

"As soon as we get out of here, we'll check them out," said Frank.

"If we get out of here," Joe replied impatiently.

It was another thirty minutes before Joe and Frank were interviewed. They gave their statements to the police officer and left the diner quickly.

Joe got behind the wheel of the van and turned to Frank. "Where to first?"

"We go to D. Sandler at twelve-forty-three Messing Road."

They stopped in front of a six-story apartment building. Examining the directory, they found that D. Sandler lived on the sixth floor.

Frank rang the bell, and they were buzzed in immediately. As they rode up in the elevator, Frank said in a worried voice, "We'd better be careful, Joe. This Sandler didn't even ask who we were. Maybe he's been expecting us?"

"I thought the same thing," Joe replied. "Let's just take it real easy."

They rang the bell of the apartment. Seconds later, the door was opened by a tiny, blue-haired elderly woman. She smiled at them. "Can I help you?" she asked with a surprisingly strong voice.

"Can we talk to D. Sandler?" asked Joe.

The woman chuckled. "That's me, young man. I'm Daisy Sandler."

Frank spoke up. "Ma'am, we found a piece of jewelry with the letters *DS* on it. If it belongs to you or a member of your family, we'd like to return it."

"Well, isn't that sweet of you. But you're wasting your time. I'm my family, and the only piece of jewelry I own is this cameo." She touched a brooch that she wore on her dress. "Sorry, boys."

Next, Joe and Frank drove to a housing development in Bayport Heights. They stopped the van before a neat, white-shuttered, colonial-style house.

Frank rang the bell while Joe stood off to the left. A bald-headed man with a crooked smile opened the door. He wore a paint-stained sweatshirt, torn jeans, and dirty white tennis shoes.

"Are you D. Sandler?" Frank asked.

"Daniel Sandler, yes. How may I help you?"

"We found a gold tie clasp that we think may belong to you. If it does, we'd like to return it."

The man smiled. "You two young men are very honest," he said. "Most people would just have kept it."

"Then it's yours? You've lost a tie clasp?" asked Frank, the disappointment plain in his voice.

"Oh, no," the man said. He reached inside the

108

house and held out a clerical collar. "I haven't worn ties for twenty years." He smiled at them. "They don't go with the collar."

As they drove to the third address, Joe said in an irritated voice, "This is turning out to be a waste of time."

"There's still one more to go."

"Let's get it over with," Joe said. "Remember, we've still got to meet Horner later on."

They stopped in front of a small frame house on a tree-lined street. A large German shepherd came racing over, carrying a ball in its mouth, which he dropped at Joe's feet. As Joe backed up, the dog reared up on its hind legs and put its forepaws on his chest. After licking Joe's face wildly, the dog bounded back on all fours, nudging the ball with his nose.

"He wants to play," said Frank.

Joe bent down, picked up the ball, and tossed it high into the air. The dog leapt after it, catching it in his mouth. He brought the ball back to Joe, dropping it at his feet.

"Looks like you found a new friend," said Frank.

Joe knelt before the dog and stroked his back. "Good dog. Get the ball." He tossed the ball down the street, and the dog raced after it.

The brothers walked to the frame house and knocked on the door. A tired-looking woman with brown hair opened the door.

"Good afternoon, ma'am," Joe said politely.

"Hello," replied the woman. "What do you want?"

"We found a tie clasp—" Before Joe could finish, the woman gave a cry.

"Oh, thank you," she said excitedly, her eyes lighting up. "My son lost it last week and was very upset about it."

"No offense, ma'am," Joe said. "But could you describe it?"

"I certainly can. It's gold and has the initials DS in diamonds on it."

"That's the one. Is your son at home? We'd like to speak to him personally."

"No, he's not. He's at work."

"Can we speak to him there?" asked Frank.

"I'm afraid not. He's a chauffeur and works for Mr. Kenneth Whippett. He usually has very late hours." She looked at Frank and Joe. "Can't you just give the clasp to me? I'll see that he gets it."

Joe gave the woman his most charming smile. "We know that. But we haven't brought the clasp with us, so we might as well come back when your son is here."

The woman smiled back at Joe. "I understand," she said.

"What time does he usually come home?" asked Frank.

"Late. Sometimes midnight," said the woman. "But he said he'd be home tonight by eight."

"Do you mind if we come back then?"

"No, I don't. David will be so happy that you found his tie clip."

Back in the van, Frank looked at Joe and grinned. "It's just like Dad's always saying. Solid investigative skills usually pay off with good results."

"We still don't know if he's one of the guys who attacked Nolan," cautioned Joe. "But that name Whippett sure sounds familiar."

"It should," Frank said. "There was a newspaper article the other day linking him to illegal gambling in this area."

"Then it all makes sense," Joe said. "As you said before, when we were talking to Nolan— Horner owes the gamblers and now they're putting pressure on him to pay up. That could explain why Nolan was attacked. Or maybe they're afraid he'll expose their operation."

Frank nodded thoughtfully as Joe pulled away from the curb. Then he said, "You know what? I think we should pay a little visit to Phil Cohen."

"What for?"

"Phil's a whiz at electronics, and I hear he has some great new equipment. Maybe he can wire us for sound before we go to Horner's room. That way we can get it all on tape."

"You're a devious guy, Frank Hardy," Joe said, turning his eyes from the road to grin at his brother.

"Look out, Joe!" Frank cried as the German shepherd dashed in front of the van.

111

14 Wired for Sound

Joe turned the steering wheel sharply to the right. The van swerved, narrowly missing the dog. Joe hit the brake hard, causing the van to skid.

The van jumped the curb and plowed into a tall hedge. Joe looked for his brother, but Frank had been thrown to the floor.

"Frank!" yelled Joe.

"I'm okay. What did we hit?"

"Just a hedge, I think. Did you see the dog?"

"I lost sight of him after you swerved."

Both brothers scrambled from the van and searched for the German shepherd. Joe got on his knees and looked under the van, but the dog wasn't there. He stood up and scratched his head. "Where is he?" he asked. "I just saw him."

"He's got to be around here somewhere," said Frank. His eyes scanned the neighborhood. "Maybe he got scared and ran home."

Just then, a rubber ball rolled to Joe's feet. Seconds later, the dog ran up and pounced on it, barking happily. Joe breathed a sigh of relief as the dog rushed over to him. Burying his head in the animal's side, Joe hugged and patted the dog, who yelped with delight at all the attention he was getting.

Suddenly, Frank tackled Joe, knocking him hard to the ground.

"Hey, what are you—" cried Joe.

"Look!" Frank pointed.

The silver sports car came from the opposite direction and pulled slowly into the driveway of the house Frank and Joe had just left. A man got out of the car and entered the house. It was too far away to see the man's face, but the white streak in his hair was unmistakable.

Minutes later, he came back out and raced for the car. The car screeched away in the direction it had come from. Luckily, the driver hadn't noticed the Hardys or their van.

"Looks like he's our man," said Frank.

"That ties David Sandler in with this case. Do you think he saw us?"

"It's unlikely. His mother probably told him that we'd found his tie clasp. He'll be lying low now."

"I don't know about that," Joe said doubtfully. "This guy acts like he's the only person in town. He and his partner attack Nolan in broad daylight. Then they destroy his trailer with a firebomb. He tries to kill Nolan in the hospital. Then he shoots at us in the diner. I don't think this guy is much afraid of anything."

"I get your point," Frank said. "We'd better be super careful from now on. Is that dog okay?"

"He's fine," said Joe.

"Let's get out of here."

Joe got behind the wheel of the van and carefully steered it backward until they were past the German shepherd. Then Joe shifted gears and they sped away.

When they got to Phil Cohen's house, they found their friend in his garage workshop, sitting at a personal computer. He looked up at them and smiled.

"Hi, guys," he said. "What can I do for you?"

"We're on a case and we need your help, Phil," Frank said.

Phil nodded. "What do you need?"

"Can you put microphones on us that will record as well as receive what is said?"

Phil scratched his chin and thought for a minute. "That's pretty complicated," he said finally.

Joe groaned. "You mean you can't do it?"

"I didn't say that. All I said was that it was complicated. But it just so happens that I have exactly what you're looking for." He held up a tiny microphone, the size of a quarter, and attached a long thin wire to it. "Put this under your shirt, Joe."

Joe fumbled with the microphone and got

114

tangled up in the wire. "How do I do this?" he asked in frustration.

Phil laughed. "Wear it like a necklace. There's adhesive on the back of the mike. Stick it to your chest."

"I've got it," said Joe as he attached the mike.

Walking to a bank of electronic equipment, Phil flicked a couple of buttons and fine-tuned a large knob. Satisfied, he turned to Joe. "Okay, say something."

"What do you want me to say?" asked Joe, and the sound erupted from four wall speakers that Phil had in each corner of the garage.

"How's that?"

Frank was excited. "Perfect. Just what we need. You're a genius, Phil."

Phil smiled. "Thanks."

"How about recording the sound?" asked Frank.

"Watch this." Phil connected a cassette deck to a receiver and adjusted the dial once again. "Go ahead," he said. "Say something." He flicked a switch.

"Will this work?" asked Joe.

The sound levels on the cassette recorder jumped as Joe spoke. Phil rewound the tape. He pressed the playback button and Joe's voice came through in a crystal-clear reproduction.

"This is just what we need," Joe said. "Do you mind if we borrow your equipment?"

"Yes, I do mind," Phil said. "You can't borrow it."

Frank's smile froze on his face. "Why not?"

"I can't lend it to you. The equipment is expensive and it's very delicate. Do you know how much that microphone you're wearing cost me?" He added, "Besides, you don't know how to work the equipment."

"Can you operate it for us from here?" asked Frank.

Phil shook his head. "No way. The microphone's range is too short."

"Look, Phil, we won't hurt the equipment. We only need it for a couple of hours," said Joe.

"I said I wouldn't lend it to you," replied Phil. "But I'll set it up in your van and operate it if you take me along with you."

"I don't know about this," Frank said. "What we're doing could be very dangerous."

"If I can't come, you don't use the gear."

Frank and Joe looked at Phil. "I don't know, Phil," Frank said again, shaking his head.

"Look, do you guys know what a boring summer I've had? I need a break. You guys are always doing something interesting. I'd like to get involved."

"You may not want to be when we tell you what's going on," Frank told him.

"Try me," challenged Phil.

Frank filled him in on the case. Phil listened carefully. When Frank finished the briefing, he smiled at his friend. "Still interested?"

"Definitely!"

"I can't talk you out of it, can I?" said Frank.

"Not a chance. Is it a deal?"

"Deal," said Frank.

"Great! Now, if we're going to get to Horner's by six, we'd better hurry. This equipment will take at least an hour to set up in your van."

When Phil had finished setting everything up, he said, "Now, for one more test. Walk outside, Joe. Count to ten, then say something."

"Okay," said Joe.

Phil checked all the wires and examined the power sources for his receivers.

"How does it work?" asked Frank. "What's your power source, batteries?"

"Yes," Phil said. "They have enough power to run the amplifiers and receivers for twelve hours without a charge. Plenty of time for what we want to do."

"I'm out here in the driveway," said Joe through the speakers.

"Good," Phil said with a nod. "Everything's working perfectly."

Joe got into the van, and the three of them headed for the Bayview Motel. The Bayview was a rundown motel on the edge of town. Its only selling point was that it overlooked the bay. Even though it was the middle of summer, the motel had few guests.

Joe parked the van where it was out of sight of Horner's room. Then he and Frank reviewed their strategy.

"I'll go in first," Frank said. "You and Phil stay with the van. If Horner's there, I'll come out and wave to you. When I do, you come over, Joe. We'll keep him talking for as long as we can.

When we get enough information we'll leave." Frank turned to Phil. "Are you sure that this stuff will work?" He pointed to the listening equipment.

"It'll work. I've got fresh batteries in the equipment and a ninety-minute blank cassette. I even put a voice-activated stop on the recorder when we came over here."

"What's that?" asked Joe.

"It means that when there is conversation, the tape will be activated. If there's no conversation, the recorder stays off. That way we don't waste any tape."

"Sounds good." Frank opened the door of the van. "Okay, here goes."

Frank left the van. As he got closer to Horner's room, he noticed something strange. "Horner's door is open," he said into the microphone in a low voice. "I'm going over to investigate."

Frank approached the room slowly, staying close to the building. When he got to Horner's room, he stopped by the doorframe and peered inside. He saw the bearded man cross the room. Before Frank could back away, he was pulled inside and thrown to the floor. He heard the door of the room slam shut. And looked up into the barrel of a pistol belonging to David Sandler.

Sandler smiled at Frank. "Nice seeing you again, kid." Then the smile vanished from his face. "Get up," he snapped.

"What are you doing here?" Frank asked as he got to his feet.

Sandler motioned toward the bed. "We're paying a little visit to our friend Zeke Horner. Isn't that right, Zeke?"

Frank looked over at the bed. Horner was sitting on the floor beside it, tied up, with a gag in his mouth.

"What's the matter, Zeke?" taunted Sandler. "Cat got your tongue?" He gave a nasty laugh, then turned to Frank. "You couldn't stay out of this, could you, kid? Well, now you're going to pay for it. You're coming with us."

"Where are you taking me?" Frank asked.

"You're going to meet my boss."

"Kenneth Whippett?"

Sandler stared at Frank. "You're a smart kid. Too smart for your own good. I wonder what else you know."

"I know enough."

"As far as I'm concerned, you know too much," Sandler said. "But it doesn't matter." He smiled. It wasn't a nice smile. "You won't be around to bother us much longer."

15 Horner Confesses

Joe watched in dismay as his brother Frank and Zeke Horner were forced into the rear of a dented green van by David Sandler and the bearded man. The green van pulled away from the motel. Joe started up the Hardys' van, keeping a discreet distance behind them.

"I hope they don't do anything to Frank on the way to Whippett's," Joe said in a worried voice. Then he called to Phil, "Raise the sound on the speakers, I've got to hear everything that's being said."

"Okay," Phil replied.

"Stay cool, Frank," Joe said between clenched teeth. "I'm on my way."

Frank looked at Zeke Horner, who was chewing on his lower lip. He was sweating, and Frank

120

could see that he was very nervous. He was still tied up, but the gag had been taken out of his mouth so that he could breathe more easily.

"What did you do to get your friends so mad, Horner?" asked Frank.

Zeke Horner didn't reply. Instead, he just glared at Frank. He shifted his position, trying to make himself more comfortable in the cramped van.

"Tell him, Horner," Sandler said. "No need to keep it a secret, right, Max?" He turned to the bearded man, who nodded and said, "He won't be alive much longer, anyway."

"You've got a smart mouth, Sandler," Horner said.

"Getting touchy, aren't you? Don't forget, I got the gun."

Horner grunted. "If only my hands weren't tied . . ."

"You still wouldn't do anything. You're all talk."

"How did you get involved in all this, Horner?" asked Frank.

Horner laughed. "For the money. It was great. I was in the majors, pulling down big bucks. I wore the best clothes. Ate at the best restaurants. I did everything. But it got expensive. My baseball money wasn't enough."

"So you started gambling," Frank said.

Horner looked at him in surprise. "Right. How did you know?" Frank didn't reply and Horner said, "Oh, right, Nolan. Well, it doesn't matter anymore."

"Go on," urged Frank, hoping that Phil and Joe were following them and were close enough to hear what Horner was saying.

"Anyway," continued Horner, "one day I lost ten thousand dollars."

"In one day?"

"On one race. I had a tip that this horse couldn't lose. The odds on the horse were fifty to one. It was a sure thing. So I bet it all."

"What happened?"

"He was disqualified for bumping another horse in the stretch. I was in real trouble. And I had to make good on my bet. I borrowed money from loan sharks to pay off the bet. When I was slow making my payments to them, they started to lean on me."

"What did they do to you?"

"Two guys met me after a game. They were carrying baseball bats, and they wrecked my car. Put dents in the doors and broke all the windows. When they were finished, one of them told me that I had twenty-four hours to pay them back or the next time they would wreck my body."

"Why didn't you go to the police?"

"I couldn't go to the cops, kid. I was a professional athlete. If word got out that I was gambling, then my career would be ruined."

"So what did you do?"

"That night in my hotel room, I had a visitor. A professional gambler and loan shark named Kenneth Whippett. He told me that he would cover all my debts if I would do him a favor."

"He wanted you to fix a baseball game," guessed Frank.

"That's right. Nothing dramatic, just a walk here and there. Not enough zip on my fastball. That kind of stuff. We still won the game, but by only one run. I didn't see anything wrong with it."

"But it was cheating," said Frank.

"Cheating who? The fans? No, kid, all I did was cost some gamblers a few dollars. I didn't regret doing it. You know, a big-league pitcher burns out his arm real quick. What was I going to do when I lost my fastball? I needed some protection."

"But it didn't stop with that one game."

"No. I thought it was a one-time-only deal. But a week later, Whippett was back. This time he wanted me to lose. I didn't like the idea. But he had me. He threatened to expose my gambling to the baseball commissioner. I went along with him."

"How much did he pay you?"

"Five thousand dollars a game. Next season I was doing great. I won my first ten starts. Then Whippett asked me to fix another game. I refused. But I pitched a bad game. Nothing worked. I gave up seven runs by the second inning. Next morning there was an envelope waiting for me with ten thousand dollars in it."

"Whippett thought you threw the game."

"Wouldn't you? I tried to give back the money, told him I wasn't interested in his bribes. But he

123

wouldn't take the money back. Two weeks later, he wanted me to throw another game. I ignored him and won the game big. The next day the clubhouse man told me that I had a package outside. I told Nolan to bring it in for me."

"Why did you pick him?"

"He was a kid. Had some kind of hero worship for me. Did everything I wanted him to. I didn't think anything of it. People were always sending me things. I had no idea Whippett was setting me up."

"They busted Nolan for taking bribes."

Horner shrugged. "Better him than me. He was nothing. I still had my career."

"Didn't you care that you ruined his life?"

"Sure I cared, but business was business. I had to think of myself first."

"Then what happened?" asked Frank.

"Nolan told me he was going to tell the commissioner that he had picked up the envelope for me. So I fed him some story about my mother being sick and how I needed the money real bad. He bought it."

"And took the rap for you. What happened then?"

"Whippett had made his point. I spent the rest of my career fixing some games and winning others. After I retired from baseball I started gambling like crazy. I couldn't pay Whippett back, and he threatened to kill me. So I went on the run."

"How did you end up with Nolan?" Frank asked. He already knew the answer—Spike

Nolan had told him—but he wanted to get Horner's answer on tape.

"I saw an ad for his camp in the paper. So I showed up one day and begged him for a job. He threw me out. When I threatened to expose his past, he changed his mind. He took me on."

"Why did you blackmail him?"

"I had to," Horner said. "I knew Whippett would find me eventually, and he did. So I had to come up with some money to pay him off."

"But you started gambling again, didn't you?" Frank pressed.

"Yeah, I couldn't help myself. And I lost big. I needed money quick. So I squeezed Nolan real hard."

"Too hard. He refused to pay you any more."

"Right. So I had to prove to him that I meant business. I started sabotaging the camp. Nolan got the message, and the money kept on coming."

"Why did you try to pin the blame on Tony Prito?"

"Who? Oh, the comedian. No, you're wrong about that. He was just in the wrong place at the wrong time."

Frank thought for a minute. Then he asked, "Why is Whippett trying to kill you?"

David Sandler laughed out loud. "This clown owes the boss two hundred thousand dollars. He said Nolan made him a co-owner of the baseball camp and that he would turn over his share of the profits to Mr. Whippett. The boss agreed."

"But Horner didn't pay up," said Frank.

"That's right," Sandler said. "And Mr.

Whippett got mad. He wanted Horner to be taught a lesson that he wouldn't forget."

"So you doctored that rubber ball," said Frank.

"It was a message," Sandler said. "But Horner didn't listen. He called the boss up and threatened him. Said that Nolan knew everything and would go to the cops if anything happened to him."

"And that's why you went after Nolan?"

"That's right," Sandler said. "And we would have shut him up permanently, too, if it hadn't been for you kids. Now we've got you, and soon we'll take care of your brother and those friends of yours too."

The green van turned onto a dirt road. An iron gate clanged shut behind it.

Joe had his hands full trying to follow the green van and listen to Horner's confession at the same time.

When he saw the crooks turn onto the dirt road, he stopped the van and jumped out. He was standing in front of a high stone wall.

"You get the police," he told Phil. "I'm going over this wall. Help me up."

Phil boosted Joe to the top of the wall by intertwining his fingers to make a foothold. Joe grabbed the top of the wall. He yelped in pain and fell to the ground.

"What's wrong?"

Joe held out his hands. His palms were streaked with blood. "Broken glass," he said.

"It's all over the top of the wall. Give me your shirt."

"Climb over the gate," Phil said as he pulled off his T-shirt. "It's safer."

"No," Joe said, carefully wrapping his hands in the shirt. "See that electric eye? It's an alarm. I don't want them to know I'm here. Let's try it again."

This time, Joe got over the wall easily. Phil heard a loud thump and a groan.

"Are you okay, Joe?"

"I banged up my knee, but I can still walk. Stop wasting time, Phil. Frank's life depends on you. Get help. And hurry!"

16 Escape Through the Woods

"End of the line," Sandler said as the van stopped in front of a large mansion. "Everybody out." He climbed into the back, opened the rear door, and slid outside.

He was joined by Max, the bearded man. Max grabbed Horner's shirt and pulled him out of the van. Then Sandler reached inside for Frank.

"I can walk out on my own," Frank said. "You don't have to grab me."

"Suit yourself," Sandler said. "Let's go."

Frank slid out of the van and slipped in the gravel of the driveway. As Sandler bent down to help him up, Frank butted him in the stomach with his head. Sandler hurtled backward into Max. The two of them got tangled up with one another, giving Frank the time he needed to make a run for it.

Racing past the van, Frank headed for the cover of the woods that surrounded Whippett's mansion. He hadn't gone more than fifty feet when he heard a pistol shot.

The bullet went high and wide, but it spurred Frank to run faster. He resisted the urge to look back, knowing that he had to build up a good lead before they began chasing after him.

He reached the trees and cut sharply to the right, running parallel to the mansion. The van was barely visible between the trees. Frank stopped for a minute to catch his breath. He saw Max run to one of the stone cottages that flanked the mansion. Frank could clearly hear dogs barking. Before he turned to continue his escape, he saw three dogs racing in his direction.

Changing his course, Frank ran deeper into the woods, hoping to put as much distance as possible between him and the dogs. Their baying filled the air, and Frank's blood chilled.

As he gulped for air, Frank forgot to watch where he was running and tripped over a tree root. He went sprawling into a thick bush, losing his sneaker as he fell. As he reached for his sneaker, he suddenly got an idea.

He decided to try to trick the dogs into following a false trail by dropping pieces of his clothing as he ran. The dogs would chase the scent on the discarded clothes, giving him a chance to escape. He knew it was a long shot, but it was his only hope.

Frank got to his feet and made four mini-trails on the forest floor, hoping to confuse the dogs. On the east trail he left his baseball cap. He took off his socks and left one on the north trail and one on the south. On the last false trail, he left his sweatband.

Carefully retracing his steps, Frank came to the juncture of the tracks and broad-jumped eight feet ahead. Then he ran deeper into the woods.

Joe ignored the pain of his bruised knee and raced up the dirt road. He stayed close to the woods so he could hide if anyone came by.

Up ahead, the road forked. Joe studied the heavily rutted road. Both routes had deep tire tracks and had been recently used. Kneeling down, he examined the tread marks, searching for a clue that would tell him which road the green van had taken.

He touched the tire track in the right fork. The dirt was semi-hard and crumbled under the weight of his forefinger. The dirt in the other track turned powdery at a light touch. Joe dashed down the left fork.

The sharp, flat sound of gunshots snapped in the distance. Joe froze, trying to figure out where they'd come from. Then from the east, he heard the shrill yelping of dogs following a scent. Could they be after Frank? he wondered as he ran forward.

The road turned. Up ahead, Joe could see a stone cottage. He stopped and caught his breath. Running into the woods that lined the road, he worked his way so that he could get a good view of the main house. The trees thinned and the underbrush grew less dense.

With the house plainly visible, Joe had to crawl to avoid being seen. He saw the green van with its rear doors open. Sprawled in the driveway was Zeke Horner. Every time he tried to stand, a German shepherd growled at him. Horner cringed and flattened himself on the ground.

There was no sign of Sandler or the man with the beard. And there was no sign of Frank. Studying the layout, Joe quickly realized that he could never make it to either the stone cottage or the main house without being observed.

As Joe lay still, watching, a figure came from behind the van and stood over Horner. Joe couldn't identify the person.

Suddenly, Joe heard a voice behind him say, "We'll find him. He won't get away." The voice sounded like Sandler's. Joe figured Sandler was about ten feet away. Soon he would be close enough to see Joe. He had to find a place to hide. But where?

Just then, Joe spotted a large wooden storage shed at the edge of the woods. Rakes and shovels leaned against the outside wall. Sacks of fertilizer, piled ten high, formed a wall to the right of the shed.

Joe darted through the trees and brush until he was shielded by the bags of fertilizer. Using the bags as cover, he slowly worked his way to the side of the shed.

There was a ten-foot gap between the sacks and the wall of the shed. He wondered how he was going to get across it without being seen.

He peered around the sacks. And was just in time to see Horner's guard rush into the woods, leaving the dog to keep watch. Seeing his chance, Joe dashed to the shed. The door was unlocked. He pushed it open and darted inside.

Frank slid into a shallow drainage ditch and ran down its length, hoping to throw the dogs off his trail. Shedding pieces of his clothing had delayed them. But it hadn't stopped them. At one point, when he had slowed down to catch his breath, they had charged out of a stand of trees, running straight for him. He had lost them only by vaulting a tangle of fallen trees.

The water rose in the drainage ditch, and Frank kept slipping in the muddy water. His clothes were filthy and the strong smell of rotting vegetation filled his nostrils.

He hauled himself out of the water and sat on the bank of the ditch, listening. The woods were quiet, and it seemed that he had escaped the dogs. He stood up and looked carefully around. Nothing was to be seen but the dense closeness of the trees and brush surrounding him.

A growl sounded to his rear, and he had just enough time to duck. A snarling dog leapt at him, and missed. It landed in the drainage ditch with a loud splash.

Frank ran as fast as he could without stopping.

His breath came in gulps and his heart raced, but he kept up the pace.

In the distance, a stone wall cut through the middle of a clearing. Just a few more yards to go, and he'd climb the fence to freedom. He reached the wall, found a foothold, and scrambled up, only to drop to the ground, his hands bloody from the glass embedded in the top of the wall.

He searched for a different way over and found it quickly. Beside the fence was a large tree with long branches that reached over the wall. He grabbed a low branch, winced in pain, and pulled himself up. Straddling the branch, he looked for a place to drop.

"Hold it!"

The voice stopped Frank cold, with one leg on each side of the branch. Then he began edging slowly forward. He might be able to get over the wall before the man could react. A dog snarled ferociously, and Frank froze.

"Don't try it," said the voice. "I've got two dogs here who would just love to go for your leg."

Turning toward the voice, Frank got a good look at his captor, a tall, thin man with blond, wavy hair. He wore a blue windbreaker, white polo shirt, blue jeans, and sneakers. He was holding two dogs on a leash.

"Who are you?" asked Frank.

"Don't you know?" the man said in mock surprise. "I'm Kenneth Whippett."

17 Kenneth Whippett

"Get off that tree," commanded Whippett.

Frank lowered himself and dropped to the ground, landing on his hands and knees. He looked up at Whippett.

"Now what?" asked Frank.

"Now we return to my house," Whippett said. "Come on." He pointed to a clearly marked trail that led between the trees.

Frank walked ahead of Whippett, searching for a way to escape. Up ahead, he saw his chance. A drooping tree branch hanging chest-high over the trail was just what he needed.

He pushed the branch forward as far as it would go. When he released it, it would lash back and stun Whippett.

"Let go of that branch," said Whippett.

"Sure thing," replied Frank as he dived to his left, releasing the branch. He rolled to his knees expecting to see Whippett on the ground, but the gambler stood to the left of the trail with a big smile on his face. The branch whipped harmlessly back and forth.

"Back on the path, Hardy. No more games."

Frank got slowly to his feet and walked in front of Whippett toward the mansion. As he walked he could hear the two large German shepherds snarling and could feel them nudging him with their noses. One of the dogs nipped at Frank's hand, and he pulled his hand up.

Whippett laughed. "They won't bite you unless I tell them to."

"You could have fooled me," said Frank.

"Don't get wise with me, Hardy. You're living on borrowed time. If you keep on smartmouthing me, I'll let the dogs finish you off. Let me show you what I mean." Whippett let go of the leashes.

"Crack!" he yelled.

The dogs each grabbed one of Frank's pants legs and worried the material with their teeth. Frank struggled to free himself, but that inflamed the dogs even more. One of them ripped off a piece of his pants leg.

"Break!" yelled Whippett. The dogs stopped the attack and took up positions on either side of their master. They looked very calm just sitting there, and Frank knew that he had been lucky.

Don't let him rattle you, he thought. Wait for him to make a mistake, then try to escape.

"Get going," Whippett said. "I've got some other business to take care of before I finish with you."

They walked back to the mansion and found Sandler and Max standing guard over a frightened Horner.

"You got him, boss," said Max.

"No thanks to the two of you. Can't I trust you to do one simple thing?"

"You wanted us to get rid of them, didn't you?"

"Sure I did. But not here. I don't know why I ever hired the two of you. You've botched up every job I've given you. And then you add to your stupidity by almost letting this one get away." He pushed Frank forward until he stood near Horner.

"Good help is hard to find these days, isn't it, Mr. Whippett?" Frank asked sarcastically.

Whippett glared at him. "I thought you'd learned your lesson. Maybe you need a refresher?"

"You don't frighten me," Frank said. "You don't think you're going to get away with this, do you?"

Whippett smiled and nodded. "I don't *think* I'll get away with it, I *know* I will."

He looked at Frank and Horner and shook his head. "You shouldn't even be here, Hardy, but Horner had to play games. He messed up my baseball camp, and now he's going to pay. And so

136

are you, because you're a witness. Get them out of my sight, Sandler," he ordered.

Stall him, thought Frank. Keep him talking. "Wait a minute. There's one thing I don't understand. Why did you just call Nolan's baseball camp *your* camp?"

"It *should* have been my camp," Whippett said.

"How can that be?" Frank asked.

"Well, since you're going to be history real soon, I might as well tell you," replied Whippett. "It was a brilliant plan, if I do say so myself."

Whippett spread his arms as if he wanted to embrace his whole property.

"Look around you, Hardy, see all of this? Gambling bought it. I do pretty well. I calculate the odds, and I figure out all the angles. Right now I'm worth about ten or twenty million dollars."

"I'm impressed," said Frank, the sarcasm thick in his voice.

Whippett's vanity made him think that Frank was admiring him. "You should be," Whippett replied. "I've got a pretty big operation. My betting parlors cover the horses and all major sports. I've got a fleet of flatbed trucks that I converted into gambling houses cruising all over the state. It's big bucks. And the demand keeps growing. Things are going great. I've got more money than I know what to do with."

Frank snapped his fingers. "You were going to use the camp to launder your money," he guessed.

137

"That's right," said Whippett, nodding. "I'd have Horner here deposit all my profits into the bank in the camp's name. The cops have been after me, wanting to know where my money came from. So I could say it came from my baseball camp. It would be the perfect setup and perfectly legal. Since Horner owed me two hundred thousand dollars, I could take his share of the camp as payment of his debt."

"I'm surprised that a businessman like you would let anyone owe him that much money without collateral," Frank said.

Whippett's face flushed, and Frank could see him trying to control his anger. "He lied to me. Told me he was a partner in Nolan's baseball camp. When he didn't come up with the cash, I wanted to know why. He told me that Nolan wouldn't give him his share. I didn't want to hear his excuses. All I wanted was my money."

"That's when Horner tried to blackmail you," Frank stated.

"Yeah. Can you beat that? This two-bit punk trying to put the squeeze on me. Nobody threatens me. That's why he's going to die. And you, too, for being so nosy."

"What about Nolan?" asked Frank.

"He's next. Then the slate is wiped clean. I'm still out the money, but everyone will know that you can't welsh on a debt to Kenneth Whippett. That's enough talk." He turned to Sandler and Max. "Get them out of here."

"Where to?" Sandler asked.

"Dump them in the bay. And make sure

138

they're weighted down. We don't want them coming up unexpectedly."

"Don't kill me, Whippett," begged Horner. "Please don't kill me. I'll do anything you want. Just give me another chance. Please."

"Forget it, Horner. You've had all the chances you're going to get."

Just then, the wail of police sirens filled the air, startling Whippett. He recovered quickly and snapped, "Sandler, get these two in the van. Now!"

Sandler grabbed Frank, tied his hands behind his back, and threw him into the green van. He and Max lifted Horner up and flung him in beside Frank. They slammed the door and raced to the front seat.

As the van started up, Whippett called out to them. "Use the back road out. Don't let them catch you. I'll stall the cops. Don't make a mistake on this or we'll all go to prison."

"You can count on us, boss," Sandler said.

From another direction an engine sputtered, then died out.

"What's that?" asked Whippett, turning around abruptly.

The engine came to life once again in a full-throated roar that grew louder and louder.

"It's coming from over there," Sandler said, pointing to the storage shed.

With a loud cracking sound, wooden slats flew into the air. Then a huge motorized lawn mower crashed through the wall. At the wheel was Joe Hardy.

Whippett stared at the scene, his mouth open. Sandler hit the gas pedal, and the van raced down the road.

Joe made a quick decision. Whippett wasn't important. He had to rescue his brother. Opening up the throttle, he angled the lawn mower to intercept the speeding van.

18 Catching a Shark

"Hey, watch it!" Frank shouted as the van bounced and skidded on the dirt road. Each bump tossed him into the air and he kept banging his head on the roof of the van.

Crawling on his hands and knees, he headed for the rear door of the van. He eased around and tried to open the door, but with his wrists bound he couldn't get a grip on the handle. He looked at Horner, who was slumped against a spare tire.

"Give me a hand," Frank insisted.

"How am I going to do that? My hands are tied too," Horner replied.

Frank tried the door several times, but it was no use. They were stuck in the van. He sat down, his back against the door, and waited.

* * *

Joe just barely managed to keep the mower on course. Soon he had narrowed the distance between himself and the van. If he stayed on his present course, he was sure he could block the van's escape.

The van swerved as one of its front tires struck a large rock, and Sandler momentarily lost control of the vehicle. He stomped on the brake with both feet. The van fishtailed wildly. When he released the brake, the van spun in a complete circle and slid onto the soft shoulder of the road.

Realizing the van was stuck, Joe turned the mower's steering wheel sharply and pointed the mower at the exact center of the van. By ramming the vehicle, he hoped he'd be able to immobilize it.

Ten feet from the van, Joe took his chance. He jumped off the mower and rolled head over heels to the safety of a large boulder.

Frank had been thrown forward when the van hit the rock. He landed on Horner, knocking the wind out of the former big leaguer. But the fall had also loosened the rope around Frank's wrists. Within a few moments, Frank managed to wriggle free. He tossed the rope away. Then he quickly untied Horner.

Up front, Sandler kept rocking the van back and forth, trying to free it from the soft dirt of the shoulder. Max groaned because he had bumped his head on the windshield when the van struck the rock in the road.

With both of his captors distracted, Frank saw

142

a chance to escape. "Let's go, Horner," he whispered.

Horner nodded. "Ready when you are, kid," he whispered back.

They crawled quietly to the rear door. It wasn't easy staying upright in the rocking van. When they got to the door, Frank tried the handle again. "It's jammed. I need your shoulder," he said softly.

"It's yours," replied Horner.

The two of them leaned their shoulders against the door as Sandler threw the van into reverse. Frank and Horner pitched to the floor.

Frank reached up and turned the handle. "Come on, Horner. We won't get a second chance. On three. One. Two. Three." They pushed together and the door sprang open, spilling both of them to the ground.

"Look out," yelled Horner as he saw the motorized mower racing for the van. It was less than five feet away.

Frank grabbed Horner by his shirt collar and pulled him backward.

Joe looked up just as the mower struck the van broadside with a loud grinding crash. The driver's door popped open and Sandler tumbled to the ground.

For a minute nothing happened, then a wisp of smoke rose from the van's gas tank. Sandler stumbled away from the van, holding his shoulder.

Then Joe saw Frank and Horner, staggering to

their feet. Joe stood up and yelled, "Get down! The van's going to blow!"

KABLAM!

The tremendous explosion sent dark gray smoke billowing high in the air. Angry red flames shot out from the van's windows.

Sandler emerged from the smoke and tried to run down the road, but he kept stumbling.

Joe didn't chase after him. He was too concerned about Frank. He plunged into the sea of smoke, searching for his brother.

Frank and Horner rolled down a hill, landing in a tangle of arms and legs at the bottom. Scrambling to his feet, Frank looked up in time to see someone else sliding down the hill.

It was Max. He was too dazed to put up much of a fight, and Frank easily pinned him to the ground. He tied Max's hands behind his back, using Horner's belt as a rope.

Out of the curling smoke at the top of the hill appeared another shape. Frank smiled when he recognized his brother jogging toward him.

"Am I glad to see you," Joe said.

"What happened to Sandler?" asked Frank.

"He ran down the road. The cops probably picked him up." He grinned at his older brother. "I'm glad you're okay."

"Me, too," Frank said. "Come on, let's get back to Whippett's house." He looked at Horner. "Ready, Mr. Horner?"

Horner nodded grimly. "I'm ready."

* * *

144

Chief Collig listened carefully as Frank and Joe told him about Whippett's gambling operation and the attempts made on the lives of Nolan and Horner. Phil Cohen was standing next to the chief.

"I've got to hand it to you two," said the chief. "You really got the job done."

"What about Sandler and Whippett?" asked Joe.

"My men picked up Sandler just a few minutes ago. Whippett tried to outrun one of our squad cars. He's safely in custody. Why don't you relax now? I'll give you a ride back to Bayport."

"No, thanks, Chief. We'll use our van. Can you use any of Phil's tapes?"

"We sure can. I spoke to the state's attorney and he's sure that we'll get indictments on Whippett and his men."

Chief Collig turned to Phil Cohen. "You did fine work with that electronic equipment, young man. Have you ever considered a career in law enforcement?"

"Not me," Phil said with a smile. "I'll stick to my computers."

"What's going to happen to Zeke Horner, Chief?" asked Frank.

"He'll probably go to prison. Though he says that he's willing to cooperate with the prosecutor to give him details of Whippett's operation if he can cut some kind of deal. Now, if you'll excuse me, I've got things to do. And thanks again for breaking this case."

As the chief talked to his men, Joe, Frank, and

145

Phil walked back to the Hardys' van. "So what do we do now?" Joe asked his brother.

"I say we take the evening off and relax," replied Frank. "Then tomorrow, we play baseball like we've just been called up from Triple A to the majors. What do you say?"

"I say let's do it!"

Joe Hardy danced off third base, taking a big lead. The pitcher fired a quick throw that nearly caught him.

"Stay put, Joe," yelled Frank, who was coaching third. "Let Biff handle it. He's had two hits today."

But Joe didn't listen to his brother. He kept increasing his lead, waiting for the chance to steal home. When Biff took a second strike, Joe knew he couldn't wait any longer. If Biff missed one more pitch, the game was over. Biff took a mighty swing and punched the ball foul over first base. Joe noticed that the pitcher was paying attention only to the batter. He was ignoring Joe. The pitcher went into his stretch, and Joe broke for the plate as the ball streaked toward the batter.

Biff stepped into the pitch, lifted the ball high, and sent it zooming over the right-field fence. A home run. Team A had beaten Team B in the baseball camp's graduation game.

The students crowded around Biff Hooper, congratulating him for his game-winning blast. Through the throng of people and well-wishers, Spike Nolan sought out Joe and Frank Hardy.

"Great play, Joe," said Nolan. "You forced the pitcher to deliver that ball earlier than he wanted to."

"I had great teachers," said Joe.

Nolan was silent for a minute.

"We heard you were offered a coaching job with a major-league team," Frank said. "Are you going to take it?"

"No. I'm not going back to the pros. I like working with teens."

"Are you coming back to Bayport next summer?" Joe asked.

"You bet I am. And you two have an open invitation. No tryouts necessary. Look, the barbecue is going to start in a few minutes. I'll see you there." Nolan turned and walked away.

After a few steps he stopped. He turned back to face Joe and Frank. "I owe the two of you a lot. You gave me back a reputation that I lost, and saved this camp. I can never repay you."

He hesitated for a moment, then reached into his pocket. He pulled out a battered, dirty baseball and flipped it to Frank.

"What's this?" asked Frank.

"My way of saying thanks. It belonged to my father and it meant a lot to him. It was very special to me too. Take good care of it."

Spike Nolan hurried away as Frank studied the ball.

"It's pretty beat-up, isn't it?" said Joe.

"It sure is. The seams are unraveling and it's all scuffed up." Frank turned the ball over in his hands. His eyes widened in surprise. "Hey, Joe, there's writing on this. And listen to what it says! 'To Gilbert Nolan, who caught my home run.' It's signed by Babe Ruth!"

"The greatest player in baseball history," Joe said. "It was nice of Spike to give us that ball."

"He's a nice guy," said Frank.

"You're right," agreed Joe. "Spike is the type of guy who proves the rule."

Frank looked at his brother. "What rule?"

Joe grinned. "Nice guys definitely finish *first!*"